VILLAGE

OF

SCOUNDRELS

BASED ON A TRUE STORY OF COURAGE DURING WWII

BASED ON A TRUE STORY
OF COURAGE DURING WWII

VILLAGE

OF

SCOUNDRELS

MARGI PREUS

AMULET BOOKS, NEW YORK

Library of Congress Cataloging-in-Publication Data

Names: Preus, Margi, author.
Title: Village of scoundrels: a novel based on a true story of courage during WWII / Margi Preus.
Description: New York: Amulet Books, [2019] | Includes bibliographical references and index. | Summary: In the 1940s, remote Les Lauzes, France, houses Jews, unregistered foreigners, forgers, and others who take great risks to shelter refugees and smuggle them to safety in Switzerland.
Identifiers: LCCN 2018058722 | ISBN 9781419708978 (alk. paper)
Subjects: LCSH: World War, 1939–1945—Underground movements—France—Fiction.
| CYAC: World War, 1939–1945—Underground movements—France—Fiction. | Refugees—Fiction. | Jews—France—Fiction. | World War, 1939-1945—France—Fiction. | France—History—German occupation, 1940–1945—Fiction.
Classification: LCC PZ7.P92434 Vil 2019 | DDC [Fic]—dc23

Text copyright © 2020 Margi Preus
Illustrations copyright © 2020 S. M. Vidaurri
Edited by Howard W. Reeves
Book design by Hana Anouk Nakamura
Title type design by Kay Petronio

Printed and bound in U.S.A.

10 9 8 7 6 5 4 3 2 1

Amulet Books are available at special discounts when purchased in quantity for premiums and promotions as well as fundraising or educational use. Special editions can also be created to specification. For details, contact specialsales@abramsbooks.com or the address below.

Amulet Books® is a registered trademark of Harry N. Abrams, Inc.

ABRAMS The Art of Books
195 Broadway, New York, NY 10007
abramsbooks.com

THIS IS A FICTIONAL STORY INSPIRED BY
REAL EVENTS AND THE EXPERIENCES OF REAL
PEOPLE WHO LIVED OR WERE SHELTERED IN
A CLUSTER OF VILLAGES IN SOUTH-CENTRAL
FRANCE DURING WORLD WAR II.

"THE OPPOSITE OF GOOD IS NOT EVIL; THE OPPOSITE
OF GOOD IS INDIFFERENCE. IN A FREE SOCIETY
WHERE TERRIBLE WRONGS EXIST, SOME ARE
GUILTY, BUT ALL ARE RESPONSIBLE."
—RABBI ABRAHAM JOSHUA HESCHEL

CAST OF MAJOR CHARACTERS

A

Pastor Autin (oh-tanh)—one of the Protestant pastors in Les Lauzes

B

Monsieur Boulet (monh-syeur boo-lay)—director and houseparent of the Beehive

C

Céleste (say-lest)—high school student originally from Paris who becomes a courier for the resistance

Claude; Clo-clo (clode; clo-clo)—Jules's friend who helps paint the roadway

Madame Créneau (mah-dahm cray-no)—organizer of the network that finds safe places for refugees on the plateau and smuggles children and others to Switzerland

D

Madame Desault (mah-dahm day-zo)—rescues children from the camps and brings them to Les Lauzes by train

F

Jean-Paul Filon (zhonh-pole fee-lonh)— Jewish teen who seeks shelter in Les Lauzes and becomes a master forger. He is also known as Otto and Jean-Paul Lafour.

H

Henni—a German Jewish teen released from Gurs internment camp to Les Lauzes, Max's girlfriend

J

Jules (zhul)—ten- or eleven-year-old goatherd who passes messages, creates diversions, and delivers forged papers for

Jean-Paul Filon. Also known as La Crapule (lah crah-pul)—The Scoundrel.

L

Léon (lay-onh)—brother of Sylvie; teen resident of Sunnyside who joins the resistance

Louis XIV (loo-ee kah-torz)—King of France, 1643-1715. Devoutly Catholic, he abolished the rights of the Huguenot Protestants, and encouraged his "dragoons" (soldiers) to persecute them until they emigrated or converted.

M

Madeleine (mah-deu-lehn)—Henni's friend, Jewish teen living at The Beehive

Max—Henni's German Jewish boyfriend, whom she met in Gurs, a concentration camp, primarily used for internment

Monsieur and Madame Mousset; M. and Mme Mousset (monh-syeur and mah-dahm moo-say)—a farm couple who offers a space to Jean-Paul Filon where he can both live and run his forgery operation.

P

Officer Perdant (per-danh)—plainclothes French police inspector sent to "keep an eye on" the townspeople of Les Lauzes

Marshal Pétain (pay-tan)—head of the collaborationist Vichy government in southern France after Germany occupied northern France. When Germany occupied southern France in 1942, he became a puppet of the German military adminstration.

Philippe (fee-leep)—high school student from Normandy who hides refugees and smuggles people to Switzerland

S

Sylvie (seel-vee)—Léon's sister, high school student and forger

PRONUNCIATION GUIDE

Pronunciation notes:

zh = the sound g makes at the end of "garage"

eu = the sound in the middle of "should"

onh = the beginning sound in "on" before you say the "n"

ah = the beginning sound in "all"

kh = the sound an angry cat makes

PLACE NAMES

A

Alsace—ahl-zahs

Annecy—ahn-see

B

Bastille (historic French prison)—bahs-tee

C

Cévennes—say-ven

Château de Roque—shah-toe deu rock

Chemin du Dragon—sheu-manh du drah-gonh

Clermont-Ferrand—clehr-monh feh-ranh

Collonges-sous-Salève—co-lonzh soo sah-lehv

D

Dunières—du-nyair

L

Le Chambon—leu sham-bonh
Le Puy—leu pwee
Les Lauzes—lay lowz
Lyon—lee-onh

M

Marseille—mar-say

N

Nice—nees

R

Rivesalte—reeve-salt

S

Saint-Étienne—san-teh-tyenn

T

Triangle de la Burle—tree-angleu deu lah burl

V

Vichy—vee-shee

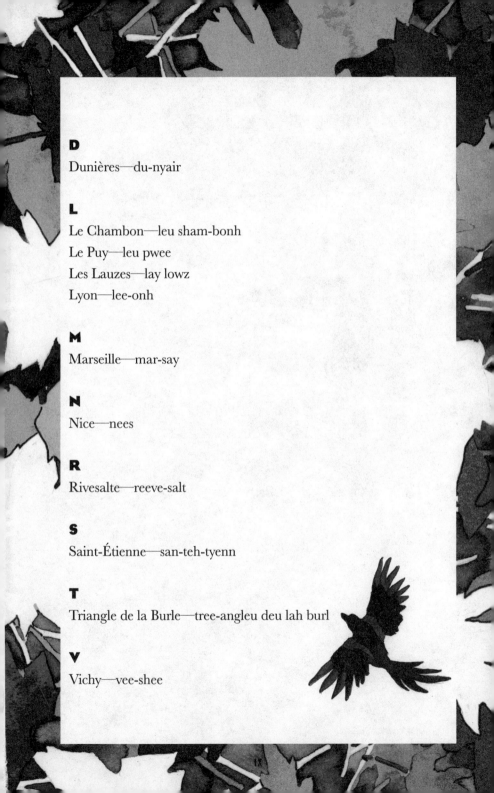

I.

EARLY MAY 1943

LES LAUZES, FRANCE

V FOR VICTORY

Jules carried the brushes. Claude, because he was bigger, lugged the can of paint. The two boys kept to the far side of the trees lining the road, trying to stay out of sight.

"German soldiers walk along here sometimes," Claude whispered.

Jules swept his gaze up and down the road and to each side. "Well, they aren't here now," he said. A faint jangle of bells caught his attention, and he turned to see a herd of goats coming out of the forest onto the road behind them.

Jules tapped Claude on the shoulder and jabbed his thumb in the direction of the road. "Here," he said, and the boys crept from behind the trees onto the roadway.

"What about them?" Claude pointed at the animals clip-clopping along the pavement. "And the old lady?" A woman in a long skirt hobbled behind the goats, urging them along with a stick.

"Don't worry about any of that," Jules said. "Now, you paint '1918.'"

"Doesn't eighteen go before nineteen?" Claude asked.

"Yes, usually, but this time paint *19*, then an *18*—that's all—because it's the year."

"But it isn't! It's 1943!"

"Yes, I know that, but . . . Never mind. I'll paint 1918. You do the *V* for *Victory*."

Claude bobbed his head happily and put brush to pavement, ignoring the goats that clattered past. But when the goatherd passed by, he looked up and whispered, "Why does that lady have a suitcase strapped to her back? Oh, is that the Ameri—"

"Shh!" Jules hushed his friend. "Make that *V* bigger. It's too little."

Once the goats were past, all that could be heard was the scrape of the brushes on the pavement and the boys' earnest breathing, a little from the exertion of the hike and from bending over to paint. And that other thing: fear of getting caught.

Jules was just putting the finishing touches on his work when he heard shouts.

"*Achtung!*" Then, "*Garçons! Arretez!*—Boys! Stop!"

Jules leaped up and tugged at Claude's sleeve. "*Vite! Vite!*" he cried, then dashed away.

He could hear Claude clomping along behind him, and behind Claude the clanging of metal-heeled boots on the roadway. Only German soldiers had boots that sounded like that, Jules knew. He glanced over his shoulder to see a couple of soldiers chasing them—still far enough away that Jules wasn't worried about getting caught. The boys only had to duck into the forest that lined the road and take any one of a number of paths and they'd lose the soldiers in no time. He glanced back again—now Claude was loping in the wrong direction—back toward the soldiers.

"Claude!" Jules shouted.

"The paint!" Claude yelled over his shoulder.

The goats skittered sideways as the soldiers ran past them.

"Leave it!" Jules hollered.

There was no way Claude could retrieve the paint and get away before the soldiers reached him.

Jules clutched his head in his hands. There was the woods, right there—full of paths leading in all directions. But there was Claude, about to fall into the hands of the Germans, the Germans who would turn him over to that policeman, Inspector Perdant.

Jules let his arms fall to his sides and ran back toward his friend.

2.
EARLY DECEMBER 1942

INSPECTOR PERDANT ARRIVES

Five months earlier, in December 1942, plainclothes inspector Perdant had arrived in the village of Les Lauzes.

The village, situated on a high plateau, was accessible from the valley only by a single winding road or a comically small train. Ever since France's surrender to Nazi Germany in 1940, the place had been living in its own little way, outside the rules of the current government. It had taken a while for that to be noticed. But now it had.

By the time Perdant arrived, winter had settled in, and the streets were snow-covered and slippery. Since the village was built on the side of a steep hill, this could make for treacherous going.

He was mincing his way to the café across from his hotel when a loud, sustained shriek made him stop in the middle of the street. Someone in danger? Distress? Perhaps his brand-new job as the sole police officer was about to begin with something truly dramatic. He turned his head—all his senses alert. Maybe one of the illegals said to be hiding here was trying to murder someone! If he could just pinpoint where the scream was coming from, he would dash to the rescue.

The high, keening "Eeeeeee" transformed to a squeal of "Aaaahhhhh," and . . . did he detect an element of glee in that scream?

The sound grew closer and clearer—like a train engine echoing between stone walls, now muffled, now screaming, now rounding a corner, gathering speed.

Then, there! Careening at high speed down the street, aimed straight at him, came a train of sleds, ridden by teenagers. Surely they'll stop, Perdant thought.

He flung up his free hand, palm-first, as if he might stop them by sheer force of will. Quickly realizing that they couldn't possibly stop, he lunged out of their way at the last moment.

"Ooohhhh!" the riders screamed as they rocketed past him.

No sooner had one sled gone by than another followed, and then another. A cap blew off, a glimpse of red stockings, a hair ribbon, snow-frosted eyeglasses. Did that boy just stick out his tongue as he whizzed past? A little brown-and-white dog chased after, barking and barking. The squeals of delight echoed between the village shops, then changed tone when the teens zoomed past the town square. Sparks flew from the metal runners as the sleds clattered over the railroad tracks, and the screams faded as the riders rounded the corner and headed toward the bridge that spanned the river.

A year or two earlier, he might have been sledding down the hill with them, Perdant thought. But now he was twenty-two and a policeman and had to look more seriously at these things.

He knew the town was full of teenagers. They came from all over France to attend some kind of "exceptional" high school meant to "promote peace and international unity." A little too late for *that*, Perdant thought. Many of these students lived in boardinghouses; it was known that some of them were foreign Jews. It was suspected that there were also communists and other illegals and undesirables. And since he was also quite sure it was not legal to ride sleds down the main street, there were obviously delinquents among them.

"Scoundrels!" Perdant said aloud before he stepped into the café, notebook under his arm, ready to begin his first report.

THE SLEDDERS

Across the bridge and a little way up the hill on the other side, the sleds slowed. One by one the sledders jumped off and stood up, brushing the snow off their jackets and cloaks, laughing and chattering as they waited for everyone to finish the run.

Philippe came careening down the the hill, leaped off his sled while it was still moving, ran alongside and jumped on again, finishing the run facing backward.

There was a smattering of applause with mittened hands, which Philippe acknowledged by standing and doffing his cap, revealing a shocking abundance of red hair.

Next came two sleds moving in tandem. First, Léon, with his feet hooked into the sled behind him that carried his sister, Sylvie.

Then a sled carrying two girls zoomed down and toppled over. The girls rolled off, and Henni stood up, but Céleste found she couldn't. Her scarf was snagged on the runners.

"Who was that man?" Henni asked, shaking her hat free of snow.

"What man?" Céleste tugged at her scarf. "I had my eyes shut the whole way!"

"The man standing in the middle of the street," Henni said.

"He must not be from around here," Philippe said, "because he didn't know enough to get out of the way."

Céleste extracted her scarf, and the group moved their sleds off the bridge to get out of the way of the last stragglers. Once all the sledders were accounted for, they started back up the long hill, and the story of the man in the street came out in bits and pieces.

"He's a policeman," said Léon.

"But no uniform," Céleste pointed out.

"Plainclothes," Léon went on. "His name is Perdant." (This elicited giggles, because the word in French meant "loser.")

"Why is he here?"

"Sent to keep an eye on us. On the town. And the area."

Henni's French had improved enough that she could keep up with the conversation and ask hopefully, "A gendarme?" The gendarmes, at least the ones who'd come around the previous summer, had seemed mostly harmless.

"He's French, not German, but he's not an ordinary gendarme. He's from the national police," Léon explained.

Talk stopped. Their breath hung suspended in frosty white clouds. For a moment, the town seemed wrapped in silence.

"National police," Philippe said quietly. That was a serious kind of police, and not as friendly as the gendarmes who showed up from time to time to arrest someone but mostly sat in the café drinking coffee and talking loudly about whom they planned to go after. By the time the gendarmes went to make the arrest, that person—no surprise—was usually long gone.

The sledders continued up the hill, each of them absorbed in their own thoughts. For a while all that could be heard were their feet crunching on the snow, and the *shoosh* of the sleds following behind.

"Gotta go," Philippe said without further explanation. He walked away, head down, knowing that what he was supposed to do later that night had just gotten considerably more dangerous. His heart raced a little, a feeling he'd become so used to, he'd kind of grown to like it.

Henni's heart raced, too, unpleasantly so. Her memory had flown to her old home in Germany. The marching soldiers in the streets, the smashing of the windows in her mother's shop, the ringing of jackboots on the stairs, only one hour to pack their things, the misery of the internment camp. Was it going to start all over again? She mumbled goodbye and trudged toward the Beehive, the house where she lived now, full of kids who really didn't need one more thing to worry about.

Céleste watched the others scatter and wondered over all their secrets. Daredevil Philippe, for instance. He was like a smoldering fire—both attractive and dangerous—composed of warm coals that seemed to burst into flames on the top of his head. She imagined the snow melting under each purposeful step he took. He was up to something. She just didn't know what.

And there were brother and sister, Léon and Sylvie, whispering to each other as they turned their footsteps toward

Sunnyside, their boardinghouse. Tall Léon bending down to self-assured Sylvie, her mittened hand gesturing. What were they talking about?

Everyone in this town had secrets. Everyone but her, Céleste thought. But what could she do? She was bright enough to do well in school, but not a genius. She was not big and strong, but as small as "*une petite puce*—a little flea," as her father still called her. She was also a scaredy-cat.

Céleste fumbled with the top button of her coat, trying to close it against the falling snow, then noticed her coat was buttoned up wrong. How could she be trusted to do something secret and dangerous when she couldn't even button up her coat right?

Still, the cold pellets tapped against her head more and more insistently. *Go, go, go,* the snow seemed to say. *Do, do, do.*

PARTY PREPARATIONS AT THE BEEHIVE

Henni stomped the snow off her shoes before she entered through the front door, then brushed the snow from her coat and hung it up. She turned to see Madeleine's head sticking out from the kitchen door, tears streaming down her face.

"What happened?" Henni said. "Why are you crying?"

Madeleine wiped her eyes on her apron and said, "Onions."

"Onions?" Henni said.

"I'm grating them," Madeleine explained. "For the latkes. Don't you remember? We're getting ready for the party. We won't have time to do everything tomorrow." She took Henni's arm and pulled her into the kitchen, which seemed to be, like the house's name suggested, a hive of activity, presided over by Monsieur Boulet, the house director.

It all looked so festive and, she realized, a little bit miraculous. It hadn't been so long ago that these kids had been barely human—that one, standing at the sink scrubbing potatoes, and that one, polishing a menorah, and that one, whit-tling a dreidel.

They'd come here thin as rails or with bellies swollen from malnutrition. Some had shaved heads or shorn hair to rid it of lice. With closed mouths and watchful eyes, with crushed spirits or lashing out in anger, they'd arrived, bedraggled little creatures.

Hunger and deprivation had at first turned them into scavenging rodents—some of them swiped food whenever the opportunity arose. Two boys she knew had crept into a neigh-bor's barn and sliced hunks off a side of bacon hanging from the rafters—Jewish boys, stealing bacon! That's how hungry they were. Henni herself had not been above sneaking into the pantry, lifting the lid off the tin of chestnut butter, and gouging out fingersful of the sweet, honey-thick paste.

Now here they were with shining faces and glossy hair, smil-ing, being courteous to one another. How had this transfor-mation occurred? In part, it was thanks to food. Not a lot of it—nobody had a lot of food anymore—but real farm food, cheese and bread, milk, sometimes butter. Cabbage and len-tils and potatoes and, best of all, jam—glowing purple blue-berry; rosy strawberry; dark, seedy blackberry—made from fruit they'd picked themselves.

Their transformation was also due to Madame Desault, who'd rescued them from the French concentration camps and who, as a Jew, risked her own life every trip up the mountain to bring them here. And to the kind guidance of Monsieur Boulet.

The day she'd arrived, Madeleine had greeted her and said,

"The houseparents are kind." Then she whispered in Henni's ear, "You know some of them are also Jewish. You'll go to school at the high school, and everyone will be your friend."

"But my French is not very good," Henni said.

"Well, that is how it will get better!" Madeleine said, laughing.

Since then she'd seen how the adults kept their young charges busy with storytelling, singing, long hikes in the mountains, and hunting for berries, mushrooms, or pine cones for winter fuel. And with schoolwork, of course.

Now, inhaling the smell of onions, Henni felt a horrible gnawing at the pit of her stomach. Like hunger, but deeper, more insistent, more aching.

"Maybe we should cancel the party," she whispered to her friend.

"No!" squawked Madeleine. "Why?"

"There's a policeman in town," Henni said. "An inspector. From the national police."

"Well, let's not invite him!" Madeleine said.

"He doesn't have to know what we're doing," someone else piped up.

"It just seems a little dangerous," Henni said.

Monsieur Boulet looked up from sweeping, adjusted his glasses, and said gently, "Do you remember why we celebrate Hanukkah?"

"We remember the miracle of the oil to light the candelabra in the temple," one of the children said. "It was only supposed to last one day, but it lasted eight."

M. Boulet nodded. "Hanukkah celebrates the miracle of triumph against overwhelming odds," he said. "Maybe it would be good to remind ourselves of that right now?"

"I suppose," Henni whispered. It would be good to remember that miracles *could* happen, because it looked like they were going to need one.

PATH OF THE DRAGOON

It was foggy when Inspector Perdant stepped out of the café into the chill of the evening air. Falling snow blurred the edges of the stone houses and buildings and veiled everything beyond the end of the block.

He shivered a little and tucked his head down into his jacket collar to begin the short walk back to his hotel.

He'd managed to strike up a friendly conversation with a pleasant fellow—a blacksmith—who sat at the bar peeling roasted chestnuts. He'd asked if the man knew a certain house located on the Chemin du Dragon. What did he know about its inhabitants?

"I don't know anything about who lives there," the blacksmith said, "but I can tell you about the Chemin du Dragon—the path of the dragoon." He slowly worked at peeling the dark brown shell away from a creamy-colored nut.

After a few moments, Perdant, anxious to get on with his questions, said, "I'd like to know."

"That road gets its name from the king's soldiers."

"The king?" Perdant said.

"Louis XIV," said the blacksmith.

Here we go, Perdant thought. Now I'm going to hear stories from the 1600s!

"You know that the Huguenots—French Protestants—were persecuted during that time," the blacksmith continued.

"Yes, I know," Perdant said. "I am a Protestant myself."

The man lifted his eyebrows in acknowledgment. "Well, back then, many Huguenots came here, to this remote plateau, hoping to escape the terror they suffered at the hands of the Catholics."

"Yes, yes, of course," Perdant said.

"The people here are descendants of those Huguenots."

"Yes, I *know*," Perdant said impatiently. This was getting him nowhere. "But all that happened a long time ago."

The man let out a little *bof* through pooched lips as if to say, *Maybe, maybe not.*

"Then Louis XIV sent his most despicable soldiers—his personal dragoons—the nastiest psychopathic killers he had— to hunt down the Huguenots." The fellow had finished peeling the chestnuts and now slid the plate toward Perdant, offering them to him.

Perdant shook his head. Chestnuts, as far as he was concerned, were food for livestock.

"The dragoons were encouraged to loot, steal, and abuse the inhabitants of the homes," the man went on, "to terrorize them until the Protestants either fled or converted to Catholicism."

"Yes, I *know*!" Perdant said, openly exhibiting his disgust at the direction of the conversation. "But that was three hundred years ago! It doesn't have anything to do with what's going on *now*."

"No?" the man said, gesturing with the chestnut in his hand.

"If you are suggesting that I am like a dragoon, you have it all wrong," Perdant protested. "I've been sent to *protect* you, not persecute you."

Again, the man let out a little puff of air, this time accompanied with a shrug of his shoulders.

Changing tacks, Perdant said, "I thought you were going to tell me something about the Chemin du Dragon, the *street*."

"Ah, yes," said the blacksmith. He rested his elbows on the bar and lowered his voice, and Perdant leaned forward, hoping that the next part would be the payoff.

"It is said," the fellow whispered, "that on foggy nights on the Chemin du Dragon, you can sometimes feel a sudden breeze, as if horses are riding past, and hear the jingling of a dragoon's spurs. Some have said they have even seen a ghostly dragoon astride a white horse."

Perdant heaved a sigh and said, "I thought you good Huguenots did not believe in ghosts."

"Of course *I* don't!" the man said. "I am just telling you what others say."

>> <<

Now, thinking about that story as he walked the dark streets, Perdant tucked his head farther down into his jacket—the cold had a bite to it. He resented the suggestion that he, himself, was like a dragoon. "*Ça n'a aucun sens*—What nonsense!" he said aloud.

He stopped and looked around and realized he didn't recognize these buildings. Between the fog and mulling over that silly story, he'd become disoriented. He must have turned the wrong way a few blocks back, or maybe gone too far, but it became apparent that he was walking the very street he and the blacksmith had so recently been talking about: the Chemin du Dragon.

Standing there, trying to get his bearings, he heard something odd. A metallic rattle. Almost a . . . jingling.

"Nonsense!" he muttered, walking on.

But the sound did not go away. And now he also detected a kind of humming whir. Both sounds seemed to be growing closer, getting louder. But it was the metallic rattle that made his heart feel as if it were ricocheting from one rib to another, because it sounded just like the jingling of spurs.

A gust of wind blew the wet mist into his face, and he turned his head away and closed his eyes. When he opened them again, he saw something emerging out of the fog. Something that looked like a horse and rider. Perdant clutched at his chest, feeling his heart throbbing even under his heavy coat. But as the apparition moved closer, it became apparent that it was just a bicyclist on a jingly bicycle.

"*Halte!*" he tried to yell as the rider whizzed past him. The word came out a kind of strangled cry.

The bicycle skidded on the snowy street and wobbled to a stop ahead of him.

Perdant took a deep breath, pressed his hand against his chest as if to slow his heart, and fished his flashlight out of his pocket. The beam swung along the road in front of him, illuminating the trees before settling on the rider and his bicycle.

As he walked toward the bicyclist, Perdant realized he needed a reason for stopping him. If he said, *You scared the living daylights out of me,* he'd make himself a local laughingstock right off the bat.

Well, he thought, a fit young man like this should have signed up for the compulsory work service. He would check his identification card.

"*Carte d'identité, s'il vous plaît,*" Perdant said, shining the flashlight at the young man.

Squinting against the glare, the fellow dug in his pockets and retrieved a card that identified him as Jean-Paul Filon, age seventeen.

So, the bicyclist was too young for the labor service. But Perdant wasn't about to let him off the hook yet. Then it came to him. The bicycle had no light, and it was dark. That was a ticketable offense.

"You realize you are riding at night without a light?" he said.

"Yes, you see, the light is broken," young Filon explained. He gestured to the light dangling from the handlebars. Perhaps that was what made the jingling sound.

"Well, you should have it fixed before you go riding at night," Perdant said. He scribbled out a ticket, citing Jean-Paul Filon for riding without a light.

The young man took it without a word, folded it neatly, and placed it in his wallet as if it were a gift.

"Now, walk your bicycle at night until you get the light repaired!" Perdant scolded.

The boy nodded, and Perdant watched him wheel his bicycle down the street. At the bottom of the hill, the bicyclist did something Perdant puzzled over for a long time. He kicked up his feet and clicked his heels together.

JEAN-PAUL AT SUNNYSIDE

Jean-Paul stood at the kitchen window inside Sunnyside, the boardinghouse where he was staying, and fiddled with the ticket he'd just been given by that policeman, Perdant.

The fog outside seemed to press against the window, as if someone had pinned a wool blanket to the glass. It made him feel far away from everything, especially his mother, who was—

"What do you have there?" Sylvie asked, interrupting his thoughts. Turning her head away from the sink, where she was washing dishes, she nodded at the paper in his hand.

"Oh!" Jean-Paul looked up, smiling. "It's a ticket I got from that policeman."

"You seem . . ." She hesitated. "Kind of happy about it."

"Well, I'm not happy about the policeman, but, I mean, it could have been so much worse."

"You're right," she said. "I might give you a ticket for not helping with the dishes." She snapped him with the dishcloth.

"Oh, sorry," Jean-Paul said. He put the ticket in his pocket, took the offered cloth, and started drying silverware.

Sylvie tucked a strand of blond hair behind her ear before plunging her hands back into the dishwater. "What did you get a ticket for?" she asked.

"Riding my bike without a light."

"You were riding a bike in the snow? I know you're new here, but why not do what the rest of us do? Use a sled or skis to get around."

"You use sleds for transportation?"

"Sure! They're great for getting from class to class. First-hour Italian is at the top of the hill, and second-hour English is at the bottom. So, why not? Even the teachers use them."

"Huh!" Jean-Paul said. "I don't see myself as much of a sledder, but we'll see."

"So . . ." Sylvie said. "Sorry if I'm being too nosy, but about that ticket?"

Jean-Paul picked up a platter and slowly wiped it dry. He had to make a decision about whom to trust and how much information to trust them with. "It's never bad to have a few extra pieces of paper in your pocket to prove who you are," he said. "Just in case the police question your identity. I guess you could call them plausibility papers. This one, signed by the local policeman, gives me a bit of credibility. It's worth the small fine I'll have to pay."

Sylvie was on the same page immediately. "Can I see your *carte d'identité*?"

Jean-Paul was anxious to see if it was good enough to fool

someone even in a well-lit kitchen, so he finished drying the platter, set it on the table, and for the second time that evening, pulled the card out of his pocket. He held it out so she could see.

"Mmmm!" Sylvie said, wiping her hands as she stood next to him.

Léon came into the room and looked over her shoulder at the identification card of Jean-Paul Filon.

"May I?" Léon took the card and held the paper up to the light, tilting it this way and that. "Gosh. It's so well done I'd almost—*almost* say it was real."

"What's the *almost* part?" Jean-Paul said.

"You mean you really *are* Jean-Paul Filon?" Léon asked.

Jean-Paul hesitated. He had planned to not tell anyone his real identity.

Sylvie tipped her head to look at him. "It's only that I've done a bit of forgery myself," she admitted, then, cheeks flushed, rushed on. "We're always looking for good people. I'm terrible at it, you see; there are some good people, but everybody's so busy and I thought maybe you knew someone . . ."

"Take a look at my sister's work." Léon pulled his own card from his pocket and held it out for Jean-Paul to examine.

"You did this?" Jean-Paul asked Sylvie.

She nodded.

He took a deep breath and hoped he wasn't being reckless when he said, "It's true, I'm not Jean-Paul Filon, but there *is* one. He's a friend of mine who gave me his card."

"But it has *your* picture on it," Sylvie pointed out.

"Yes, that's me."

"How did you get the seal to look so real—I mean, the part of the seal that covers the photo—how did you do that?"

"I used an art pen to trace the missing part of the official seal onto the photo."

"Well done!" Léon said.

"Have you done any more of these?" Sylvie asked.

Once again, he wondered how much to tell them. "In Nice, where I lived before, I had a job as an office equipment repairman," he said. "And I often worked at the office of the prefect."

"The prefect!" Léon exclaimed, clearly impressed. "You mean the official in charge of issuing identity cards, passports, and all things dealing with immigration issues? Go on . . ."

Sylvie and Léon leaned forward in their chairs, and Jean-Paul told them about the day he had gone to the prefect's office on a mission of his own. This was back when his name was still Otto.

He had parked his bike outside the government office buildings, unstrapped his toolbox from the back of the bike, and had gone inside . . .

"Good. You're here," the secretary said briskly, not bothering with a customary *"Bonjour"* in greeting. Then she added, her lips twisted into a mean little sneer, *"Here to* doctor *the typewriter?"*

Otto shoved his glasses up on his nose and didn't speak. He had already planned on never talking to her again.

"The g *is sticking and the* t *is blurry,"* she said. *"Change the ribbon while you're at it, will you?"*

Otto nodded. His mouth was so dry, he wasn't sure he could speak, even if he had planned on ever talking to her again.

"Well, go on," the secretary said impatiently, tilting her head toward the rear door.

Otto slunk past her into the prefect's office. There was, as he had hoped, no one in it.

He shut the door. Moving quickly but deliberately, he set the toolbox on the desk, opened it, laid out a cloth, and set his tools neatly one by one on top of the cloth, so everything would look like it usually did if anyone came in.

But instead of going to the typewriter, he went to the prefect's desk, slid open the top left-hand drawer, took out two sheets of official government stationery, and carried it back to the typewriter desk. Turning the type-writer so he would be facing the door, he cranked the sheet of paper into the roller and placed his fingers on the keys.

He paused, conscious of every little noise: The scraping of shoes on the tiled floor outside the office. A small cough. People passing by outside the window. Even the chirping sparrows trying to stay warm near the steam grate. Every sound made him flinch.

November 1942, *he typed.*

To the immediate attention of the director of Rivesaltes Internment Camp . . .

A heavy door slammed down the hallway. He stopped, waited a moment, then resumed.

This document authorizes internee Eva Grabowski to be released from Rivesaltes, effective immediately. The aforementioned is to be permitted to travel to her place of residence. Please refer to the enclosed residency permit.

Otto pulled the newly typed sheet of paper from the typewriter and set it aside, then inserted the second sheet into the roller. From his pocket, he pulled out his own resident permit and set it next to the typewriter and carefully began to copy the words.

With the keys clattering away he didn't hear the door open. He didn't hear anyone step into the room.

"Otto?"

His head came up. Madame glared at him, her lips pursed.

"Oui?" he croaked, his fingers floating above the keys.

There was a long moment—was it long? It seemed to last forever—when everything in the room felt as if it were suspended on strings, including his fingers, hovering just above the keys—and it would take only a couple of words to sever the strings and everything would come crashing down.

"Are you soon finished?" she asked rather curtly, obviously irritated by his lack of an earlier response. "I'll be needing the typewriter."

"Almost," he said. Forcing himself to smile, he added, "Madame." He had often wished he could say to her, If it weren't for the Germans and the Vichy laws, I'd be at university right now, studying to be a doctor, and one day you might have worked for me as my secretary. Then you would have to call me "Doctor," and "sir," and I wouldn't tolerate rudeness!

"Fine, then," she said, backing out and closing the door.

Otto waited until his hands stopped trembling, then finished his typing. The document completed, he cranked the roller to release the paper and carried both pages to the prefect's desk. A quick glance over his shoulder confirmed that he was still alone, so he opened the stamp pad, picked up the prefect's stamp, and stamped first one, then the other, document.

As for the hardest part, the signature, he could do that at home. He rolled up the documents and put them and his tools in his toolbox, latched the box, and was almost out the door when he remembered the blurry t *and the sticky* g. *He had to force himself to go back to the typewriter, where he quickly made the adjustments on the offending keys, and, even though there was still plenty of well-inked ribbon, exchanged the old roll for a new one. He tucked the used roll of ribbon into his toolbox.*

And, well, why not? Since he was in it this deep already . . . he reached over and snagged one of the prefect's stamps and stuffed that into his toolbox. He snapped the clasps on his box, exited the office, and strode out quite confidently, giving a nod to the secretary as he closed the door behind him.

"Well?" Sylvie asked expectantly.

"Well, what?" Otto, now Jean-Paul, said.

"Who is Eva Grabowski?"

"My mother," he said.

After a moment, Léon asked, "The letter—did it work?"

Jean-Paul nodded.

Léon and Sylvie leaned back, relieved, and Sylvie asked, "Where is your mother now?"

"She is . . . safe," Jean-Paul said. There was a limit to how much he would tell.

Léon let out a low whistle. "You're good," he said.

"More important," Sylvie said. "Can you do more documents?"

"If I can get my hands on some tracing paper and the right kind of ink . . ."

"Come with us," Sylvie said.

The threesome went up the stairs past the girls' floor and up another flight of stairs to the boys' floor, where they walked down the corridor, passing rooms on either side. The boarders looked up from their desks or beds, then back down at their books and notebooks as the three new friends went by.

Jean-Paul wondered if there were others who, like him, were Jews hiding from the authorities. Probably likely, but hard to say for sure, because it seemed to be an unspoken rule in this house not to speak about your background or religion.

Passing a cubbyhole-size room, he saw what looked like an unruly tangle of red hair sticking out above the covers.

"That's Philippe," Sylvie whispered. "He goes to bed early."

They climbed one more flight of stairs to a small attic, crowded with a few file cabinets and a desk with a typewriter on it.

"The teachers use this as a sort of office," Sylvie explained. "Since there isn't any actual school building, they have to use whatever space they can find for classes and office space."

Léon opened a cupboard that held a variety of colored inks and different kinds of paper. Jean-Paul caught a glimpse of something that looked like blank ration cards.

"What do they use these different colored inks for?" he asked, running his finger along the bottles in amazement.

"You have to have the right color inks for the different kinds of documents—and from different government officials."

"Are you telling me," Jean-Paul said, "that the *teachers* are forging documents?" Had he stumbled into a den of criminals or some kind of forgery utopia?

"Not *all* of them," Léon said. "But some are quite talented. The secretary is very good at forging signatures, for instance." He rubbed his hands together and said, "So . . . let's see what our *new* talent can do."

Jean-Paul's fingers twitched with anticipation. "Leave me alone and you'll see," he said. "In half an hour I can copy even a complicated official seal."

"You're on!" Sylvie said while Léon retrieved a document with an original seal from their local prefect. He handed it to Jean-Paul and said, "Good luck."

Jean-Paul gathered together paper, ink, and pen and sat down to work. As carefully as a surgeon sutures a wound, he began to copy the seal. His art pen was his needle, the ink was the thread, the paper his patient.

All his focus was on his work. He didn't—couldn't—think of anything else. Not the war or its injustices, not where his father was or whether he was still alive. All he could do was concentrate on the task before him: the precision of the line, the perfection of the circle, the flourish of the signature.

It was oddly thrilling, this work. He was good at it. Quick, sure, steady-handed. *And*, he thought, holding the paper up to examine his handiwork, *artistic*.

After a half hour, Léon and Sylvie came back, examined the document he'd made, and proclaimed him a genius.

"We should discuss where to keep all this." Sylvie spread her hands, indicating the materials. "With that policeman in town, this house could be targeted for searches. We're going to need to find a different place to do this work."

"Let's discuss it tomorrow," Léon said, yawning. "I'm going to bed."

Sylvie agreed, and the two of them headed to their respective floors.

»«

Jean-Paul couldn't sleep, so he continued working on something harder: copying the signatures of regional officials. His imagination was fired—until now he hadn't really thought that his skills could help others. All his energy had gone to saving himself and his mother.

When he and his mother had arrived in Les Lauzes less than a month earlier, he was no longer a Latvian Jew named Otto, and she was no longer his mother. Thanks to Otto's talents with a pen, he was now Jean-Paul Filon, a seventeen-year-old French student from Alsace, and his mother had been transformed into a middle-aged Turkish-Russian spinster named Mademoiselle Varushkin.

When they had first arrived in Les Lauzes, he had parked the weary mademoiselle in a café and gone to check out the town. Right away, he noticed that the people who passed by didn't scowl at him or cross the street to avoid him. There were no propaganda posters like the ones he'd seen elsewhere in France that depicted Jews as hideous-looking monsters trying to take over the world.

He stepped into a bakery and used a ration coupon to purchase a loaf of bread. The shopkeeper didn't close the door before he could enter. She didn't look past him to see if there was someone more suitable she could be serving. She didn't ask him where he'd come from. She simply served him politely, and with a pleasant smile handed him his purchase.

It was as if the people in this town hadn't heard that everyone was to be suspicious of everyone else now. As if the news hadn't reached them that neighbors spied on neighbors, turning in people over old slights, insults, grudges. As if they hadn't heard that they were to be leery of people who looked like they might be Jews.

The butcher had a few sausages; the greengrocer had a bushel of potatoes. Someone cycled by with a huge wheel of bread slung over his handlebars. The village had food—not a lot, maybe, but some. The village seemed to have decent people. The village also had a policeman. The very one who had given him, Jean-Paul Filon, a ticket, signed and dated—something like a little gift—legitimizing his name and status.

He pulled it out of his pocket and looked at it again. There was his name, written by the policeman himself. He was marveling at his good fortune when he heard the creak of the stairs and the soft thump of a door closing downstairs.

Who was going out at this hour of the night, he wondered. He switched off the light and went to the window.

The fog had cleared, and the sky, now inky black, was spattered with stars. Snow blanketed the sleeping village, the streets, the roofs.

Against the white snow, he made out the darker figure of a person—one of the students. When the boy came out from the shadow of the house, Jean-Paul caught a glimpse of curls just before a stocking cap was pulled over them. It was that redhaired kid, Philippe, who went to bed early.

Jean-Paul watched as Philippe took one of the long wooden sleds that leaned against the side of an outbuilding and walked toward the center of the village, dragging his sled behind him on the snowy street. What *was* he up to?

There is something very unusual about the people in this town, Jean-Paul thought, not for the first time.

PHILIPPE AND THE "TRAVELERS"

The streets were empty, the windows dark. Only the crunch of Philippe's feet and the *whoosh* of his sled runners against the snow-packed street disturbed the quiet of the sleeping village.

He tucked his sled out of sight in the narrow space between the buildings, then gave a quick glance over his shoulder before climbing the stairs to a second-floor flat.

Going to see Madame Créneau was like going to a nice aunt's house—a nice aunt who gave you a bite to eat, fussed over your health, and who was also forging documents and involved in clandestine activities.

She wore soft blouses and straight skirts and sensible shoes— as one must when there's so much walking to be done. Her small flat was kept tidy, and no matter what else, there was always a hot cup of something for you at Mme Créneau's.

"I'm sorry it's not *real* coffee," she apologized as she pressed a mug of hot liquid into Philippe's hands. "At least it's hot."

He murmured his thanks and couldn't help glancing behind her into the kitchen.

Mme Créneau didn't miss the glance. "Did you sleep through dinner at your house again?" she asked, stepping into the small kitchen.

"I guess I did," he said apologetically.

"Don't do that!" she scolded as she cut into a loaf of rye bread. "You've got to keep up your strength."

"You know there's a policeman in town," he mumbled over the mug.

Madame spread soft white goat cheese on a slice of bread and nodded. She turned back, holding the sandwich out to Philippe while giving him a little cautionary shake of her head. One that said, *Let's not talk about that right now.* Philippe took the sandwich as she smiled at someone behind him.

He turned to see his "travelers," as he thought of the people he guided. Tonight it was a young couple with a little girl. All three wore woolen coats; the man had a hat, the woman a wool scarf over her head, and the child was so bundled up that only her watchful brown eyes shone out from her swathing of scarves. Like her parents, she was quiet, alert, and, he could tell, worried.

Maybe a joke would help.

"Hey, you know why they bury Nazis twenty meters underground?" he asked.

They shook their heads slowly, not sure if he was telling a joke or not.

"Because deep down they are really nice!"

The little girl's dark eyes crinkled at the corners above her scarf—she was smiling. Philippe couldn't help but smile back.

He swallowed the dregs from the mug and handed it to Mme Créneau, then stepped outside. For a moment, he stood just outside the door and listened for the sound of cars or motorcycles. Only about three people in the village had a car—now four, since the policeman probably had one—and could get gas to drive it. So if you heard a car, you suspected police or military. But the village was silent—especially as it was muffled by snow.

Philippe motioned for the others. Onto his ample sled he piled their meager belongings: a battered suitcase, a box tied shut with rope, a muslin sack stuffed with who knew what. He set the little girl in the midst of these things, and off they went, the parents walking alongside while Philippe pulled the sled.

Once again, the only sounds were the *shoosh* of the metal sled runners and the whining of the snow under their feet. Philippe couldn't help but compare the quiet here to the sounds of the German army rolling into his hometown in Normandy.

Even though that had been almost three years ago, he still vividly remembered the officers on horseback, the horses' hooves clattering and ringing on the cobbled streets. Tanks, roaring and rumbling, shaking the ground under his feet. Then row upon row of square-shouldered, crisply marching soldiers, the stamping of their boots like rolling thunder. The rows of soldiers stretched on and on, every one of them tall and blond and square-jawed, each with a rifle on his shoulder, in shiny leather boots and high-collared jackets. They seemed as invincible as gods, and Philippe had almost wished to join their ranks . . . until he remembered they were the enemy. A heart-clutching fear set in—there were so many! They were so well equipped! They were so disciplined! How could anyone fight them? Yet—and he felt the first fizz of excitement when he realized it—he knew that, somehow, he would.

But the armies had not come to this little corner of France. Not yet. And because the armies hadn't come, the refugees had.

Soon Philippe and his travelers left the village, following the road into the countryside of open fields and dark swaths of forest. It was a clear night, and the cold cut right through their wool layers. A few stars and a sliver of a moon shone through the trees. The earlier fog had settled on every twig and branch; then the temperature had dropped, creating hoarfrost. Now the trees sparkled in the moonlight.

From her perch on the sled, the little girl pulled her scarf away from her mouth and chirped, "It's like a fairy castle! And there's a party. Listen!"

Philippe and the girl's parents stopped to listen to the ice-covered branches and twigs clicking against one another.

"Can you hear the silver spoons and crystal goblets clinking and clattering?" the girl asked.

Philippe looked at her parents, noting the sad slope of their shoulders, their slowly nodding heads. Perhaps they were recalling dinner parties served on their own crystal and silver—now likely in the hands of others.

"It's like magic, isn't it?" the little girl finished.

It was magical, Philippe agreed, but magic that could turn

dark in a moment—like a crystal goblet unexpectedly shattering into dangerously sharp shards.

He listened again for the sound of motors. Nothing. Through the trees, the solemn voice of an owl seemed to call out the time—*Two. It's two.*

They set off again, walking up the road for a time until striking off onto snowy hillsides. Though the parents were quiet, from time to time the little girl remarked about something—a tree shaped like a hobgoblin, a boulder that looked like a dog sitting on its haunches.

"I see a consternation," she piped up, her head tipped way back to regard the sky.

Philippe looked up. "A constellation?"

"Uh-huh," she said. "How many stars do you think there are? More than five million-million?"

Philippe waited for her parents to answer, but they were silent, lost in their own thoughts.

"Tonight," he began, and then suddenly remembered something he had learned in school. "Tonight there are more stars in the universe than grains of sand on all the beaches in the world. We can't see all of them, of course, we only see . . ." Philippe racked his brain, trying to remember the number of stars that could be seen on any given night. "I guess it's only a few thousand."

"And every one as beautiful as the next," said the girl.

The shape of a farmhouse and barn appeared fairly close at hand, and Philippe guided the family into a nearby grove of trees. He held up his free hand, signaling the others to stop, and stared at the stone farmhouse, its windows dark. *Please let a light appear*, he prayed.

The cold was sharp as a razor, he thought, glancing at the refugees' hunched shoulders, their chins tucked into their collars. Like knives, stabbing them through their coats. If the farmer didn't light a lamp, Philippe would have to shepherd his charges back to the village, a more dangerous endeavor now that there was a policeman to consider.

But, then, there it was: the glimmer of lamplight through the lace curtains. Philippe felt a rush of warmth, as if the heat from the lamp reached all the way to their circle of trees.

"Come on," he said. "Coast is clear."

The farmhouse door opened; Philippe shooed the refugees in as fast as he could and followed them inside. He stayed just long enough to warm his hands and belly with a cup of hot tea. Then it was back into the cold, alone.

He pulled the sled to the edge of the steep hill leading down toward the village. Then, in anticipation of the stinging wind, the sled runners singing against the crusty snow, and the thrill of the dark ride ahead, he launched himself and his sled over the edge and into the night.

AN IMMENSE HOPE

The next day, Inspector Perdant's second night in the village, he meandered along the streets, trying not to look like he was peeking into windows. Evening was descending, and the wooden shutters on the windows were being pulled shut one by one, so he turned his steps toward his hotel. But when at one of the houses he thought he heard singing, he stopped.

He stared at the house. The music sounded suspiciously Jewish. Yiddish. Or Hebrew-ish.

Should he investigate? Although his official job description was to "maintain positive relationships with the locals," he knew the *real* reason was to identify evidence of illegal activities and unregistered Jews, communists, and undesirables.

He took one step, then stopped. Maybe he was imagining it. The sound was very faint. Ever since he'd practiced shooting a Sten gun, he'd had a little ringing in one ear, so there was that. Or it could be a trick of the wind whistling through the slates on the rooftops.

He backed up ever so slightly and studied the window. A soft glow emanated from behind the lace curtains, as if candles were burning inside. He made out the silhouettes of young people, and then at the window, for a brief moment, a face appeared. A girl. Just before she closed the shutters.

It wasn't strictly in his job description to bang on doors and demand entry without justification, and he didn't want to make a fool of himself so soon after his arrival. But he could pay a friendly call, couldn't he?

»» ««

Inside the Beehive, everyone had gathered around the menorah for the lighting of the candles. Henni looked around at the others, at their eyes welling with sorrow. What with missing their families and longing to be in their own homes, there was plenty of loneliness and sadness to go around. But as the blessing was sung and the first candle lit, she saw in its tiny flame, courage. In its bright spark, the potential for miracles. And shining in the eyes of her friends, hope.

Each day for the next seven days, another candle would be kindled and blessings recited. The flames would leap up, bright and strong, their light dancing in the darkness. Like us, she thought. We will be the miracles.

It was perhaps a miracle that she and the others were here at all.

Like nearly everyone new to Les Lauzes, Henni had arrived on the funny little narrow-gauge train, La Tortue—the

Tortoise—with its steam engine puffing great clouds of important-looking black smoke into the sky.

It was not a fast-moving train. Mostly, it seemed to Henni, it moved up. Up and up through fragrant pine forests or open farm country revealing vistas of the valley below: a patchwork of farms and fields, stitched together with rivers or rows of trees. The other children, most of whom were younger than Henni, were by now all cried-out and asleep, their faces still puffy and red. Henni gazed out the open window while tiny specks of soot and glittering bits of ash floated in.

The train didn't move fast, but as far as Henni was concerned, it was moving away. Away from the concentration camp at Gurs and its dark, unheated barracks crowded with starving women and children—including, still, her mother. Away from the cold muck that oozed over the tops of shoes; away from the stinking and overflowing latrines; away from the meals of thin gruel, when there was a meal; away from the desperate, all-consuming hunger.

But it had also taken her away from Max. Max, who had made life bearable in the camp. Even better than bearable.

"Max," she wondered softly now, "where are you? I hope you are safe."

As the train had moved up, the air sharpened. Every pine needle, every leaf, every blade of grass seemed polished to a high sheen. Only the faraway mountain peaks were hazy, so cloaked in blue mist that one couldn't be sure if they were there at all.

The war, Henni thought, seemed as far away as those peaks. Yet, like the mountains, always present, looming.

Madame Desault leaned forward and spoke as if casually, yet with an intensity that made Henni turn away from the window and the other children lift their heads. "Remember what I told you," she said as the train pulled into the station. "When you meet people, don't tell them much about yourselves—not your religion or the country of your birth or where your parents are." Then she leaned back while everyone sat very still for a few moments, letting it sink in: Even in this remote place, it was still important to keep certain things to yourself.

They arrived at the station and saw for the first time the town that would be their new home. On one side of the tracks, a forested hill, on the other, the village—stone houses closely nestled together, shops and streets that wound down the hill to a small river that winked and glittered as it bounded over stones and under bridges.

Here she was to live in a home with dozens of others—war orphans, children sent to the plateau to improve their health, students who attended the high school, or Jewish kids like her, plucked from the camps and brought to a place above the clouds.

Was it possible that this hardworking train that chugged so slowly up the mountainside had taken them to another kingdom, a kingdom outside the world of war? she wondered as they all tumbled out of the carriage and onto the platform. Following the rest of her group down the cobbled street, her little suitcase—all she had left of her whole life—banging against her leg, Henni wondered if perhaps they had left the war and all its cruelties behind.

But she could feel it trailing them. The war was a broken dam, a muddy flow that couldn't be stopped, and she was quite certain that some-day, somehow, it would once again arrive on her doorstep.

And now it had—in the form of that policeman, whom she could see through the window, coming up the walk.

Perdant was nearly on the doorstep of the Beehive when he heard a voice behind him. "*Bonsoir, Monsieur,*" said the voice.

He turned to see a small group of teenagers standing on the street with their ever-present sleds behind them.

"*Bonsoir,*" he said, trying to sound friendly.

"How are you enjoying our little town?" the girl asked. Her cheeks and the tip of her nose were red from the cold. Like a lot of people around here, she was wearing the wooden shoes called *sabots* and a loden cape. He didn't care for the capes. They were smelly when damp, and so voluminous that small children could be concealed beneath, for all he knew.

"Very nice, thank you," Perdant said. He wished they would go away so he could proceed with his investigation, but they continued to stand there as if he should say something. "Are you joining the party?" he asked, jabbing his thumb toward the house.

"Party, Monsieur?" the girl said.

"I thought I heard singing." He held up a finger and cocked his head.

"Singing?" The girl seemed to listen. "I don't hear anything."

"Perhaps you hear the water running under the ice on the river," one of the boys said. He pointed to the other side of the street, where, at the bottom of the hill, the river ran. "It can sound like human voices singing. Sometimes it sounds like 'The Marseillaise.'"

All three teens began to sing the French national anthem with great gusto. As soon as they finished one verse, they went right into the next.

Perdant nodded and smiled at them. Then, a bit uncomfortably, his gaze drifted to their sleds, covered with lumpy blankets.

Finally, he held up a hand as if to say, *All right, I have heard enough. I get it. The river sings the French national anthem.* He tried to interrupt, but they just continued singing. Verse after verse—he'd forgotten there were so many—helping one another with the words and giggling when they forgot some of them.

At last, he gave them a nod and a wave and walked away, thinking that some of the people in this town were a little strange.

>> <<

The three young people continued singing for as long as they could see Perdant. When he was gone for good, they stood perfectly still for a moment and, hearing no more sound coming from the Beehive, walked on, pulling their sleds behind them.

Finally, Léon said, "Hey, did you hear the one about the two policemen?"

"Is this a joke?" Jean-Paul asked.

"Of course it's a joke!" Sylvie said. "That's all he knows!"

"The policemen were talking to each other on the street," Léon went on. "The first one said to the second one, 'What do you think of our new regime?' The second policeman said, 'Same as you.' 'In that case,' said the first policeman, 'it's my duty to arrest you.'"

Sylvie and Jean-Paul let out little nervous laughs. Each one tried not to let the others know just how wobbly their legs felt and how their hearts seemed to echo in the hollow vaults of their chests.

>> <<

By the time Sylvie, Léon, and Jean-Paul had reached their destination, their legs had started to function normally and Sylvie had found her natural voice again.

The farmer, Monsieur Mousset, greeted them and showed them around the farm. Typical of the area, it consisted of a stone house and barn, all connected. An inside door between the house and barn made it possible to tend the animals in the depths of winter when the snow and wind made impassable drifts outside. Of course, there were also doors leading outside.

A room off the side of the barn was to be Jean-Paul's living and work space. It was simple and small, with a bed and a desk, though no running water. No matter. In the yard outside Jean-Paul's door, spring water ran freely through a pipe into a stone trough. Maybe the best thing of all, the animals were right on the other side of the wall, helping to keep the place warm.

There wasn't really heat in the room, but it felt warm. The camaraderie and the fire of their passion for the work supplied all the heat they needed. Jean-Paul felt energized. Soon he would be doing something. Really doing something to fight the Nazis.

"It's perfect," he said, rubbing his hands together.

The farmer gave a nod and went off to tend to his chores.

"It'll be a much safer place for our operation," Léon said. "The student houses are liable to be searched—as we saw tonight!"

"That was a close call," Sylvie agreed. "It probably wouldn't have been good to have the policeman call on them right in the middle of a Hanukkah party!"

"I don't get it, though," Léon said. "Those kids came here perfectly legally. The law allowed for them to be taken out of the camps. So why is it now so dangerous for them to be here?"

Jean-Paul set a box down on the table and turned to them. "It's a gradual eroding of rights and privileges," he said. "The Nazis and their puppet government in Vichy take away rights and make new restrictions little by little, so you can't keep ahead of them. There are always new criteria for arresting people. And they're sneaky, too. Like, they tell you to register and then you'll be legal. But then they have your names and addresses and know everything about you—so it's much easier to arrest you!

"For a time it was legal to take the kids out of the camp, but now it's not so easy," Sylvie said. "The rescue organizations sometimes have to smuggle them out, I've heard. And now, if the police manage to track down the children that were taken out, they are returned to the camps in the name of 'family unity'!"

"It doesn't make any sense!" Léon exclaimed.

"Nothing makes sense anymore," Sylvie grumbled.

Slipping their mittens back on, they stepped outside to get more things.

"What if that policeman had asked to see what was under the blankets?" Sylvie said.

"Perfectly harmless!" Jean-Paul said. "Just school supplies, right? Paper, ink, stamps . . ."

"A sewing machine?" Léon asked as he and Jean-Paul hefted an old treadle sewing machine into the space.

"That would have been the easiest thing to explain—it's just a sewing machine," Sylvie said.

"But perfect for making the perforations in ration cards," Jean-Paul added.

Sylvie set the typewriter on the table.

"Careful with that!" Jean-Paul said over his shoulder.

The typewriter had been brought from Africa by a missionary friend of one of the teachers and was thoroughly convincing in its ancient, official, been-there-forever kind of way.

"Beautifully untraceable," he said, running his hand affectionately over the keys.

"The way I see it," Léon said, "there's going to be no end of need for papers. What with the roundups in the cities, more Jews and other refugees will come here."

"It has a reputation as a safe place," Jean-Paul said. "Some may find places to stay on the plateau. Many will want to keep moving, to Switzerland, if possible. All of them are going to need papers."

"Now with a policeman spying on us, even more people are going to need identification cards," Sylvie said. "They'll also need ration books, demobilization papers, birth and baptismal certificates, school diplomas, marriage licenses . . ."

"Even library cards, prescriptions, and rent receipts," Jean-Paul said. "But I think that once we get everything set up, we might be able to turn out maybe thirty, even fifty, documents a week. But who's going to deliver all these documents to the right places? I don't really know my way around yet."

"And you shouldn't spend your time hiking all over the plateau," Sylvie agreed. Pointing to the table, she added, "You should be right here."

"Don't worry," Léon said. "People have a way of turning up when you need them."

JULES

The next morning there was a knock at the door. Jean-Paul opened it to behold a boy of about ten or eleven with a puppy tucked under his arm as if he always had one there.

In spite of the cold and snow, he wore short pants and knee-high woolen stockings, with a navy blue beret pulled down on his head. The beret had a little button on the very top, and Jean-Paul had the impression that if he pressed it, he might set the boy spinning like a top.

"*Bonjour,*" the boy said solemnly.

"*Bonjour,*" said Jean-Paul. "Are you one of Monsieur and Madame Mousset's children?"

"Me?" said the boy. "No. I'm Jules."

"Well, Jules, how can I help you?"

"I was thinking," Jules said, craning his neck to try to see into the room, "that I might help *you.*"

"Jules! Jean-Paul!" Mme Mousset waved at them from the

farmhouse door. "Get out of the cold and come inside, you two!"

Jules and Jean-Paul walked across the yard and stepped into the kitchen, where each was handed a mug of warm milk. Jean-Paul's had a splash of ersatz coffee in it.

"What kind of a position are you looking for?" Jean-Paul asked Jules. "And what are your qualifications?"

"My qualifications are that I know this whole area." Still holding the puppy, Jules spread his arms wide so that the puppy kicked his legs nervously. "I know the hills, the forest paths, where the gates are on the fields. And the sheep trails. I know the farmers, too—who lives where."

"And how did you come to this vast knowledge?" Jean-Paul asked.

"I have a herd of the orneriest goats this side of the Cévennes Mountains. They run away. They hide. They get into trouble. So I meet a lot of people."

"Where are they now?" Jean-Paul asked, gazing out the window as if expecting to see them pawing at the snow outside.

"They are in the goat shed at home," Jules said, looking at Jean-Paul with the kind of pity reserved for city boys. "My little brother is taking care of them."

"Your . . . *little* . . . brother?" Jean-Paul said.

Jules nodded. His dark eyes were those of an adult's set in a child's face. Now they regarded Jean-Paul with a touch of bemused tolerance, as if to say, *Perhaps it's different in the city where you're from, but here on the plateau, we all—young and old—have to work, you know.*

"I know what you're thinking," Jules said. "You're thinking

that I'm too young. But that's what makes me perfect. Nobody will suspect me."

Madame Mousset made a little affirmative sound and added, "That's so."

"How old are you?" Jean-Paul asked.

"Ten," the boy answered.

"What about your parents?" Jean-Paul said. "Do they know what you'll be up to? And do they approve?"

The way Jules saw it, if his father could join the resistance, well, then, he could do something, too. If his mother found out what he was doing, she'd find him, drag him home by his ear, scold and chatter away like a red squirrel, and send him to bed without his supper. But he'd just climb out the window and be gone again. Eventually he'd wear her down and she'd give up—he felt sure of that.

He did not say any of that. He just said, "Oh, yes. It's fine," without looking directly at Jean-Paul.

"I wouldn't want you to get in trouble," the older boy said.

Jules laughed. "I'm in trouble all the time!"

"Serious trouble, I mean," Jean-Paul clarified.

Jules gave a little one-shoulder shrug. "Don't worry about me."

"If you were caught with papers, you couldn't say where you were taking them or who gave them to you. No matter what. You understand that?"

"*Absolument*," Jules said.

"You won't know what the documents say or exactly who they're for—only where to take them."

"*Absolument*," Jules repeated.

"I can't pay you much," Jean-Paul went on. "And by 'not much' I mean 'not anything,' at least at the moment."

"I don't do it for the money," Jules said. It was an opportunity to do something really important—and dangerous. And he hated the *boches*. He knew he wasn't supposed to call the Germans *boches* or Fritzes or Krauts or beetles—all derogatory terms—and he wasn't supposed to hate them either. He went to church and listened to the sermons. Still, his insides zinged a little and his skin prickled just thinking of getting the better of them in any way possible.

Plus, he already knew that stopping at farms often elicited a reward of a slice of meat, maybe an egg or two, some vegetables, an apple, sometimes even a piece of cake!

The two shook hands, and a deal was struck.

3.
MID-DECEMBER 1942

UNWELCOME GUESTS

For a while that winter there was little to disturb the tranquility of the small town but the *shoosh* of sled runners, the hushed foot-falls on snowy sidewalks, the tiny ticking of snowflakes against windows. Except, on this particular day, there was one noisy classroom above a bookstore near the village square.

Class had yet to begin, and students entered the shop, stomped the snow off their *sabots*, shoes, and boots and shook the snow off their jackets and wool capes before hanging them on the coatrack. Then they bounded up the stairs to their still-frigid classroom.

The teacher had not yet arrived, so the students chattered and joked while Philippe attempted to make a fire in the old, leaky woodstove in the corner. What he mostly got, though, was smoke.

"You finally come to class, and look what happens!" Sylvie teased as she made her way to the window. "I thought you were a Scout."

"Not a very good one, apparently," Philippe answered, fiddling with the metal handle that opened the flue.

"Here, I'll show you how it works," Céleste said. As she reached for the damper, their fingers touched. She pulled her hand away, blushing. Most schools were either all-boys or all-girls, like the one she had attended in Paris. She'd never gone to a coed school before, and being around boys was, well, different.

Sylvie opened the window, and Léon and Henni waved their hands to try to waft the smoke out of the room.

"*Mon Dieu . . .*" Sylvie whispered. Her voice was even chillier than the winter wind blowing in through the window. Without turning around, she waved everyone over.

A dozen heads crammed the open window and watched from their perch on the hill as, one after another, several dark green army trucks appeared on the road leading into town.

"*O la vache,*" Philippe whispered. "Holy cow."

The trucks bounced over the bridge into town, rumbled by the square, and turned onto their street.

"Maybe they're just passing through," Céleste suggested.

For those who could travel the main roads, Les Lauzes was not "on the way" to anywhere. So if there were German trucks, they were probably planning to stop.

And they did. One by one, they parked in front of the hotel across the street from the bookstore.

Henni's pulse raced. She backed away from the window. Her glance darted toward the stairs. "Are they coming here?" she asked.

"I don't like the look of it," said one of the students. "I blame the letter."

"What letter?"

"Shh," Sylvie said.

The whole class silently watched as the truck doors opened and soldiers began to emerge. Slowly. Not in any rush. Then they began to hobble toward the hotel, some of them with canes or crutches, others helped along by their comrades.

"They don't look like they're going to be conducting raids anytime soon," Philippe observed. "They look pretty beat-up." He winced a little at the sight of bandaged heads and arms in slings.

"The Germans are moving in right next door to—" Céleste stopped. Goose bumps rose on her arms as she thought of the children living in the boardinghouse next door to the hotel: twenty children, an unknown number of whom were Jewish. And the director of the residence, also Jewish.

The room hushed as others contemplated this unspoken situation.

Then one of the students chimed in, "Even if *these* Germans are harmless, having them here can only mean *more* Germans. It's the fault of the letter."

"What letter?" one of the others asked.

"This summer some of us wrote a letter to Vichy's Minister of Youth," Sylvie explained. "To voice our outrage about the roundups in Paris when thirteen thousand Jews were arrested—"

"Over four thousand of them were children. Children!" Céleste exclaimed. "All of them rounded up and put in the bicycle stadium, with no food or water . . ."

"The children were separated from their parents. The adults were stuffed into cattle cars and deported," Sylvie continued.

"Then the children, too, were put on trains and deported to Auschwitz."

"An extermination camp," Henni whispered.

"They told people it was a relocation program," said Sylvie, "but word has come from the camps about what is really going on there."

"We have to do what we can to keep those and others who reach us safe," Philippe said.

"What we said in the letter," Sylvie went on, "was that we believed the deportations would soon start in the south. And that we would not give up the Jews in our midst."

"First of all, if anyone demands that Jews register here, don't do it!" Philippe said. "The roundup wouldn't have been possible if Jews in Paris hadn't registered when the German occupiers demanded it."

Henni thought about how her family had thought they would be safe if they followed the law. They had thought of themselves as more German than Jewish. Her father fought for Germany in World War I. Surely, her mother had thought, they wouldn't come for *us*! And so they had done what the law required of them.

"I still don't see how the letter has anything to do with this," Céleste wondered. "I mean, with Germans coming here."

"The letter told the Vichy minister, and I quote," Léon said, "We want you to know that there are a certain number of Jews among us. If our friends, whose sole fault is to adhere to a different religion, receive deportation orders, we will encourage them to disobey those orders, and we will do our best to hide them."

"What?" said one of the students. "Why did you tell him that?"

"Those in power have to hear people calling them out for their immoral policies," Sylvie said. "They have to hear people saying, 'This is wrong.'"

"Why does it have to be *us?*" asked another student.

"Why *shouldn't* it be us?" Philippe answered.

"We're just kids."

"Maybe we're the only ones brave enough to do it."

"Or stupid enough," mumbled Léon.

"To say nothing is to tacitly agree with their policies," Sylvie said. "It's the same as saying that what is taking place is acceptable."

"If we don't speak out against what is wrong, we are contributing to the problem," Philippe said.

The teacher arrived and, after hanging up her coat, explained in a grim voice, "The hotel's been requisitioned for convalescing soldiers who've been wounded on the Eastern Front."

"Maybe it's not appropriate," Léon said, "but that reminds me of a joke."

"It is not appropriate!" Sylvie snapped.

Léon plunged ahead anyway. "Hitler asks a soldier at the Eastern Front what he wishes for when he is under artillery fire on the front line." There were groans, but Léon forged on. "And the soldier answers, 'I wish that you, my führer, were next to me.'"

When class ended, the students left their bookstore classroom and began walking to their next one.

"Don't worry, Henni," Céleste said, touching Henni's arm. "You're one of us now." Céleste and Sylvie stood on either side of their friend as they walked.

Henni didn't answer, because the sound of drumbeats and shouts caught their attention.

"*Avis à la population!*" the *garde champêtre* shouted, banging his drum on the street corner. The somewhat unofficial town crier wore something that vaguely resembled a uniform, though a uniform for *what*, it would be hard to tell. He was a funny little man with a black mustache that he nervously smoothed before speaking.

Villagers gathered around to hear what announcement he had to make. Céleste and her friends stopped, too.

"What now?" Céleste wondered. "More bad news?"

"What could it be?" Sylvie said. "Germany is already occupying the whole of France—so that can't be it."

"They've already instituted compulsory work service for all the young male adults. Maybe they've decided to send *everybody* to work in German factories!" Céleste said.

"First they send us a policeman. And now the Germans."

What could possibly be next?

"*Avis! Avis!* Notice! Notice!" the *garde champêtre* cried again. He banged his drum, smoothed his mustache, then announced in a loud voice, "It is forbidden to slide down the village streets on sleds!"

The three girls couldn't help it—they burst out laughing. The villagers who had been expecting some important announcement threw up their hands in disgust and walked away, back to their errands.

Henni listened with one ear to her friends discussing their evening plans—plans she knew included sledding on the village streets—but she had the distinct feeling someone was watching them, as if the heat from someone's stare was burning a hole in her back. She brushed snow from her shoulder so she could take a surreptitious glance behind her, and noticed a German soldier standing outside the hotel, looking at her.

He pulled out a white handkerchief with which he began to clean his spectacles.

Henni's skin prickled. A hard lump lodged somewhere in her chest. Her friends' voices seemed far away, their words as distant as the sound of the river running under the ice.

All she noticed was that white handkerchief.

Her mind flew to the last day she'd seen her mother that past August. She'd been sent word from Gurs, the camp where her mother was still being held, that her mother was sick and Henni should come quickly. She arrived at the camp, only to be told that it was on lockdown—no one was allowed inside. Her mother, along with many hundreds of others, was to be deported the next day. Perhaps she could see her mother then, an aid worker suggested.

It had been dark, though the summer night still warm, by the time Henni had walked the nineteen kilometers to the rail yard. The tracks were empty; warehouses lined the lonely platform. Was this it? A freight yard?

Exhausted, Henni curled up on a scrap of dry pavement next to one of the warehouses and tried to will herself invisible as rail workers slipped by like shadows. Deported, she thought again, hearing the voice of the aid worker. "East," she'd said.

East was not good. East was Poland. East was extermination camps.

The next morning, Henni awoke to a nightmare worse than anything she could have dreamed. A long line of cattle cars stood along the platform, each car filled with ghosts. Through the open doors, she saw that the cars were crammed with people, people so transparent a gust of wind might have carried them away.

If only she could do something, Henni thought. If she had a sorcerer's power to call down the fierce winds of the plateau! To call down the snows to bury the rail lines! To call down fire, lightning! If she had such power, she would do it.

She did not need to remind herself that she did not. The feeling of powerlessness overwhelmed her. She was powerless even to find her mother among so many people.

One of the gendarmes approached her. "What are you doing here?" he said.

"I'm looking for my mother," she explained.

"Do you know where she is?" the policeman asked.

"No. How could I know among a thousand people?"

"What's her name?" he asked.

Henni looked at him, wondering why he wanted to know.

"I will find her for you," he explained. "What was the number of the barracks where she lived?"

Henni told him her name and the barracks number.

He started to go but turned back. "What goes on here tears my heart out," he said, then offered her a drink from his hip flask. When Henni declined, the policeman took a swig himself, then walked away.

After a short time the gendarme returned and said, "Follow me," then led her through the crowd until they reached the car that held her mother. The gendarme helped Henni up inside.

When her eyes adjusted to the gloom, the full horror of the situation struck. The rough, wooden car was obviously meant to carry cows and pigs, not people. A few shreds of straw lay scattered about on the floor, and a single bucket stood in a corner.

"Mama?" Henni said.

Her mother stepped out of the gloom. Though it had been only a few short months since Henni had last seen her, it was as if decades had passed. Gone were the bright eyes and hearty laugh, the robust figure, the glossy hair. Her dress, her only dress, hung from her bony frame, and her hair was gray and lusterless.

Henni thought of how she'd wanted to leave Gurs, even though she'd had to leave her mother behind—and her grandmother in the cemetery there.

"I should have stayed with you," Henni whispered.

"No," her mother said, shaking her head. "It's good you left. They have taken away everything else. Little by little they took away our right to work, to go to school, to go to movies, concerts. Each time, we said, 'Now they will be satisfied—what more can they take?' Each thing must be the last, each time, the worst insult. They took our silverware and jewelry, our savings, our houses, our businesses. How was it we kept believing it would end? Finally, all that is left is our lives. And it seems they must have those, too." She clutched Henni's shoulders and whispered, "Don't let them take you."

The metallic clang of a steel door sliding shut on one of the cars startled them both.

"Go, go!" her mother said. "Quickly, before they close the doors." She peeled Henni's arms from around her waist and pushed her toward the door.

Henni backed away. People in the car helped her down to the platform. She was barely out of the car when a policeman came by.

"*You!*" *he barked at her. "What are you doing out here?*"

"*I just came to see my mother,*" *she managed to squawk.*

Behind her, she heard the loud grating squeal as the doors began to slide shut, then the heart-stopping clang as they closed with horrible finality. One after the other, after the other, after the other.

The policeman looked up at the sound, and the gendarme who had helped her earlier appeared, took her arm, and led her toward the gate.

"*Shoo!*" *he said. "Run!*"

Henni dashed outside the gate, where she turned and clung to the metal fencing. The train began to roll away, car after car filled with people: someone's father, mother, sister, brother. Finally, all she could see of her own beloved mother was a little white hankie through the slats of the boxcar, waving goodbye.

"Henni?" Her friends stood looking at her. "Henni?" Céleste repeated.

"Sorry," Henni said. The entire memory had taken only the amount of time it took for the soldier to clean his glasses. "I was just thinking about something else."

"You were miles away," Sylvie said.

I *should* be miles away, Henni thought. She had been safe here for a time; she had loved being here. She looked at her friends. They were kind. But how much longer could they protect her and the other young people sheltered here? Perhaps it was time to think about getting out.

CHRISTMAS MAGIC– DECEMBER 25, 1942

On Christmas Day the church was transformed from a drab stone building into a wonderland of flickering candlelight, perfumed with the sharp, sweet scent of freshly cut fir. Earlier that day, children watched as a draft horse dragged a huge fir tree right into the church, its hooves ringing on the granite floor, its breath white clouds of steam in the cold air.

Now the flames of a hundred candles glowed on the tree's branches, filling the church with warm light. The congregants had arrived on sleds or skis, by horse-drawn sledges, on foot. The pews were filled, children in the front with their faces tipped up to listen to the pastor, who was telling a Christmas story of his own devising.

Under the reign of Caesar Augustus, the story began, *two men lived in Bethlehem, a town in Judea. The first man was immensely rich, the second was very poor.*

Inspector Perdant tiptoed in after the service had begun and slipped into the back pew. He watched as the pastor paced back and forth in front of the tree, bouncing a bit on his toes, his bright blue eyes shining in the candlelight.

It happened that a census was to be taken, the pastor said, *and everyone in that land was required to register, each in his hometown. The rich man flung his doors wide, welcoming all strangers—as long as they could pay for their room and board, of course. He couldn't be expected to host people for free, after all!*

The poor man swept out his humble abode and waited, hoping to welcome strangers. But no one wanted to stay with him because they would have had to sleep in the barn.

Jean-Paul listened to this story from the other side of the back pew from Perdant. He'd never attended a service before, and he wasn't sure why he was here now. But as for taking shelter in a barn, Jean-Paul well knew there were people hiding this very night in barns all over the plateau. In fact, his own room was separated from the animals by a wall so thin that he was awakened every morning by the cow butting her head against it.

Céleste was thinking about what was coming next in the story. She thought she knew: Joseph and Mary would be turned away by the rich man and would end up in the poor man's barn.

Sure enough, that's how it turned out.

The poor man was thrilled to welcome them, the pastor said. *He invited them in, gave them something to eat, and prepared a straw bed for his guests.*

Henni, sitting with some others from the Beehive, knew only too well about beds of straw. She, herself, had slept on straw on the floor of the barracks at the internment camp. Just thinking about it made her shift uncomfortably in her seat, her bones remembering the cold, hard floor she'd shared with dozens of others. She thought of her mother. And all those who had been taken away on that or other trains.

That night, the story went on, *a baby was born, and since there was nowhere else to lay the babe, he was laid in the manger.*

The message of this story could be, Henni thought, you never know who might be God's child, so you should treat all strangers as if they are. But, then, aren't we *all* God's children? She remembered her grandfather saying that in each person—even the poorest, even the most unlikely—there is a divine spark. The difficult thing was to be able to perceive that spark in others—it could also be hard to see it in oneself.

Like Jean-Paul, she was a little surprised to find herself in the congregation. Sometimes she and the other Jewish kids went to services just to find out what was going on in the outside world. But nobody tried to—or wanted to—convert them. The pastor said when the war ended, they should be returned to their Jewish parents as Jews.

Looking around at the congregation, Perdant had to admit this place had the look of pure innocence. The children with their freshly scrubbed faces glowing in the candlelight, the adults listening with rapt attention, all dressed in their very best. The simple farmers, hats off, heads bowed. Their sturdy wives with their white caps tied tightly beneath their chins.

What, Perdant wondered, was going on in all those heads right now?

The farmers were thinking, Pastor Autin is encouraging us

to offer refuge to those who come to us when he says, *God did not choose the wise or the intelligent, the rich or the powerful, to manifest himself to the people of Israel. God chose the illiterate and the humble, the poor and the weak.*

What, Henni wondered, did the Nazis make of this Christian story about love for the weak and powerless? Hitler and the Nazis hated the poor and weak so much that they had begun systematically eliminating people with mental or physical disabilities, people they deemed "unworthy of life."

There must be a lot of things wrong with Christianity if you are a Nazi, Henni thought. For one thing, Jesus had been a Jew. That must rankle the Nazis no end, she thought with a little shake of her head.

Inspector Perdant was not thinking about the story at all. He was staring at the teenagers. That girl, for instance. That odd little shake of her head. What was that about? That boy next to her, when he turned his head—a handsome boy, with a face full of pathos. Perdant hated him instantly. He felt in his bones: Jew.

He'd heard that they went to services sometimes—likely to try to disguise themselves as Protestants. He'd determined that there were dozens of children's homes, some of them funded by aid organizations known to rescue Jewish children from the camps. Not all of them children, either, but old enough to be real troublemakers.

Like that row of teenagers. That redheaded kid, for one. He'd seen him once pulling his sled along in the middle of the night. What had he been doing out at that hour?

With his head bowed, Philippe unfolded the note he had

been handed earlier. It read: *Couple of Old Testaments for you.* He put his mind to the farms in the area. Where might these "Old Testaments" go?

And in that region there were shepherds out in the field, keeping watch over their flock by night, the pastor was saying.

Jules looked up, thinking, *I* am a shepherd, and I was out in the fields the other night, although I wasn't keeping watch over my flocks, I was delivering some fake papers. And while I was out there, suddenly, there was in the sky a multitude of winged angels. These actually turned out to be parachutes, drifting out of the heavens toward earth. This proved that Britain knew there were resistance groups forming in the mountains, and as far as Jules was concerned, that made for tidings of great joy. It meant that Britain, still living in freedom, hadn't forgotten France and was sending tools for its liberation in the form of canisters full of, probably, submachine guns.

Jules looked up shyly at his pastor, whom he knew to be a pacifist, and decided he would not tell him about this. But he was so excited he couldn't keep from squirming a little.

The younger children were thinking about far more innocent things. They had begun to seriously wonder about what was in the gift they would receive at the end of the service—candies and nuts? An orange or tangerine? Maybe a little puzzle, a book, or a game.

The story came to an end, and the congregation began to sing "Silent Night."

Silent night, Holy night.
All is calm, all is bright.
Round yon Virgin, Mother and child.

Holy Infant so tender and mild,
Sleep in heavenly peace,
Sleep in heavenly peace.

Henni's French had improved enough that she understood all the words, but she couldn't help but think of the last time she'd heard this carol—back in her hometown in Germany a few years earlier. By that time, Chancellor Hitler had proclaimed himself the savior of the people and had gone about changing everything, even the words of hymns. Henni had been hurrying home that Christmas Eve when she'd stopped to listen to the singing coming from the Protestant church. Then she made out the words:

Silent night, Holy night
All is calm, all is bright.
Only the Chancellor steadfast in fight,
Watches o'er Germany by day and by night,
Always caring for us.
Always caring for us.

The service ended and people began filing out. Perdant joined the slow surge of people moving toward the big double doors, where the pastor stood shaking the hands of his parishioners. All headed home to cheery Christmas meals, no doubt. Perdant would spend his holiday having dinner at the hotel and taking notes about some of the people he had observed at the service.

"Inspector Perdant!" Pastor Autin clasped Perdant's hand

in both of his. "So nice to see you here. You are a long way from home, I think! Are you alone today? Would you like to join our family for dinner?"

Perdant rocked back on his heels for a moment. This was a completely unexpected invitation. He tried to quickly weigh the pros and cons. If he accepted the invitation, he could get into the pastor's home and perhaps gather evidence of his illegal activies. On the other hand, the pastor would probably grill Perdant during dinner about *his* activities: What was he doing in Les Lauzes, what did he hope to accomplish, and so on. The pastor was probably just trying to get information out of *him*!

Not knowing what to say, Perdant said what he had earlier rehearsed: "I am well aware what's going on around here, you know. I know that there are homes full of non-Aryans and anti-patriots."

The pastor regarded the policeman for a moment. "So you are a spy," he said. "Isn't there more honorable work you could find to do?"

"One finds work where one can," Perdant mumbled before plunging out the door into the cold. Why he should be made to feel guilty for keeping law and order in this town, he didn't know.

As he struck off toward his hotel, head down, hands shoved deep in his coat pockets, he thought of what he should have said to the pastor. He should have said, "Take care, Monsieur Autin. If you aren't careful, it may be *you* whom I will have to arrest—holy day or not!"

4.
DEEP WINTER,
1942–43

LA BURLE

Snow cascaded down in torrents or drifted down one flake at a time. It draped like lace curtains or was driven sideways by wind. It fell all day, flake by quivering flake, or belligerently, in downpours, piling up into small mountains or making tall, snowy hats on stumps and fence posts.

Then came the wind, howling across the plateau, a wind so familiar it had been given a name: *La Burle*. La Burle breathed icy blasts of frigid air and pushed the ever-falling snow into *congères*, snowdrifts. Mighty snowdrifts. A farmer might emerge to find great, sparkling heaps of snow piled against his door or his hayfield sculpted into the white cliffs of Dover. Perhaps you'd wake to the Alps in your backyard or the Himalayas stretching across the main road out of town. These were the *congères*.

The *congères* closed roads. The *congères* sometimes blocked train tracks. And the *congères* kept the police and the gendarmes stuck in the valley.

The weather tried Perdant's patience. There was little he

could do without orders—and support from police headquarters in the valley—so he continued to snoop, to gather names, to ask questions, to wonder: How did Jews get here?

It was known that there were children pulled out of the camps and brought to the boardinghomes here. But they weren't the only ones. There were plenty of others. Undocumented Jews were hiding here. They were being smuggled into Switzerland, so there had to be a forgery operation. Who was running that? And where? He knew there were parachute drops—you'd have to be blind not to notice the new silk shirts on some of the children, the pretty white dress with its telltale "French fell" seams on the hotelier's daughter. That meant the resistance must be organizing in this area. Where were they hiding? Perdant meant to find out.

And who was behind all this illegal activity? Perdant suspected the pastors—all of them, but especially the two in this town. They were the ringleaders, and something must be done about that.

THE KING SURVEYS
HIS KINGDOM—
FEBRUARY 1943

In February, there was a little break in the weather. The wind stopped. The blowing snow settled. The trees stood still, every branch and twig motionless.

The villagers caught themselves whispering. Practically tiptoeing around town. Barely breathing.

The first rumble of trouble came from the snowplow, grumbling up the road from the valley. It burst triumphantly into town, growled around the streets and town square, and trundled off in the other direction, and for the moment, stillness returned to the village streets.

>> <<

Outside of town, in the countryside, Jules stooped now and then to pick up twigs and sticks and even large branches that had fallen during the winter's frequent storms. His dog got into the spirit of it by dragging along a stick as big as himself.

Jules stopped at a spot just off the road and dumped his armload of wood behind a large boulder, which would act as a windbreak for any breeze that might start up. Then he carefully laid a little campfire, leaving enough room so he could use the boulder as a backrest. One match—that was all he allowed himself, because matches, like everything else, were hard to come by these days. So he took the time to lay the twigs and sticks carefully over a scrap of birch bark he'd found.

Earlier in the evening, Jules had dropped off some papers at a farm and had been rewarded with a small sack of potatoes, a few onions, and a chunk of thickly cut bacon. He was delighted, for he'd carried in his rucksack a small saucepan and matches, just in case something like this might happen.

He piled on the sticks until the flames leaped up orange and bright—warming his face as he bent over the fire, gently adding bigger and then bigger sticks and branches.

Once the fire was sending sparks and smoke straight up into the darkening sky, he cut off a small piece of bacon, then sliced a couple of potatoes and one of the onions. The rest would go home to his mother to feed his siblings and a couple of "cousins" who were staying with them.

The flames subsided, revealing glowing coals beneath. He plunked the bacon into the pan and set the pan over the fire. As soon as the bacon had produced some grease, he threw the onions and potatoes into it, holding the handle with his mitten, which doubled as a hot pad.

By this time, the sun was gone. Beyond the circle of light his fire provided, the sky was the color of the blackest ink in the blackest bottle of Jean-Paul's collection. But Jules was not afraid of the dark. For one thing, it was rarely as dark as you expected. In winter, the snow was like an enormous, luminous blanket—as if someone had buried lanterns under it, making it glow. Often there was a moon, sometimes bright enough to cast shadows. And even if there wasn't, there were stars. Like tonight, when the stars were shining with a special fierceness.

If it was cloudy, it could be dark, but he knew his way around so well he thought he could do it blindfolded. Seeing was only one of the senses, after all. You could tell where you were by the breeze on your face, the smell of sheep nearby, the peculiar creaking of the weather vane on a certain barn, the rattle of a particular gate, or the feel of the ground under your feet.

But until you were frying bacon on a fire, the air scented with woodsmoke, you didn't think about how deprived of the sense of smell you were all winter when most smells were frozen or buried under three feet of snow.

Now the onions and potatoes were really starting to sizzle, and the aroma was so mouthwatering, he couldn't sit still. It set him to humming and doing a little jig. Partly to stay warm, partly to keep himself from eating the potatoes before they were done, and partly out of sheer excitement of the deliciousness to come.

When he tired of that, he leaned back against the boulder while the dog earnestly gnawed on a stick. He could no longer see it but still sensed the old, abandoned château that loomed not very far away. He imagined its shape—its turret and elegant roofline, tall and regal against its mountain backdrop. He imagined himself as king of that castle and that he'd been out hunting with his hounds—here he reached over and patted the wriggly little mutt next to him, still chewing up and spitting out bits of wood—and he pretended he had stopped to survey his kingdom.

But, Jules thought, not even a king could be as pleased with a meal as he was with the one he was about to consume.

Jules was deep into this reverie when he sat up with a start, realizing someone was nearby. Perhaps the crackling of the fire had prevented him from hearing the approaching footsteps.

Philippe's face appeared, illuminated by firelight. With a smile, the older boy said, "I could smell your banquet a mile away. Smells divine. Are you expecting the king?"

"I *am* the king!" Jules crowed.

"I should have recognized you, Your Majesty," Philippe said, bowing deeply.

"Would you care to join me?" Jules said. The tiny pang of regret he felt about having to share his repast was compensated by hosting the daring and dashing Philippe. Also, Philippe had a sled to sit on and a canteen of not completely frozen water. These things assured his status as an ideal dinner guest.

Once they were situated, Jules announced, "Dinner is served!"

The two of them plucked warm potatoes and onions coated with salty bacon grease from the pan with their fingers, licking their fingers between each bite. At last there was only the chunk of bacon left.

"That's yours," said Philippe.

Jules took a bite he judged to be about half and handed the uneaten part to Philippe.

"Sure?" Philippe said.

"*Bon appétit!*" Jules said, setting the cooled pan on the ground for the dog to lick clean.

Jules and Philippe settled back against the boulder, and Philippe said, "That was a feast fit for a king."

"Well, like I said . . ." Jules said, "I *am* the king. And that"—he pointed to the barely visible outline of the château—"is my castle."

"And where is your crown?" Philippe asked.

Jules pointed up at the sky. They both tilted their heads to gaze at the brilliantly shimmering stars.

After a moment, Jules's gaze returned to the dark outline of the old château. "I used to play in there when I was a kid," he said, as if he were now an old man.

Philippe raised an eyebrow. "When was that?"

"Back when I had fewer responsibilities," Jules said. Then he leaned toward Philippe and whispered, as if there might be someone listening, "I know the château's secret."

"Oh?" Philippe whispered back. "What's that?"

"Well, it's a secret," Jules said. "But maybe I'll show you sometime."

They sat for a moment, and then Philippe said, "I have bad news. The pastors and the director of the school were arrested."

"*What?*" Jules sat up, sending the dog skittering away.

"Today," Philippe continued. "Five police cars came to arrest the three of them."

Jules stared into the fire, as if there might be an explanation in the flames.

"Word got out," Philippe said. "People came and brought them little gifts: a tin of sardines, a jar of jam, a package of coffee, a candle. When Pastor Autin said he didn't have any matches, one of the gendarmes fished a box of matches from his pocket. 'A gift,' he said."

Finally, Jules asked, "What will happen to them?"

"They're to be taken to a kind of internment camp for political prisoners."

Jules wished he would have been there. He could have given Pastor Autin his matches. The bacon, or the potatoes, the onion. Nobody ever got enough to eat in those camps.

He poked at the glowing coals with a stick, getting that prickly feeling in his head that meant he was about to cry. Trying not to by clamping his mouth tight and squeezing his eyes shut just made it worse, and when Philippe put his hand on the younger boy's shoulder, the tears rolled down and his nose began to run. He couldn't have said why he was crying: because the most admired men in the community were the ones who were arrested? How could that make any sense at all? Sometimes it seemed as if the world had gotten turned upside down, and Jules didn't know if it would ever get turned right side up again.

He hoped Philippe couldn't tell he was crying. Then he heard Philippe sniff and, taking a shy glance, saw bright tears sparkling in his friend's eyes, too.

"Why?" Jules managed to choke out.

Philippe sighed. "I suppose the authorities want to silence them because they speak out against the Nazis and the Vichy regime. And we listen to what they say."

"The Nazis are afraid of the pastors because the pastors are right and they are wrong," Jules said. "And they know it."

Philippe nodded. "You speak truth. We need more kings like you."

The fire had died to small flames, and though it still warmed the front of him, Jules felt the cold sneaking down his neck and creeping up under the back of his jacket. He felt his heart thudding away, really realizing that what he had gotten involved in was not a game, not a lark. It was serious, dangerous business.

"Perhaps it's not so safe anymore, what you've been doing," Philippe said softly.

Jules shot him a glance. Firelight reflected in Philippe's eyes. Or maybe, Jules thought, he was catching a glimpse of the fire that seemed to burn within the older boy.

"I don't care," Jules said with a shrug. "They want us to be so afraid we give up. If that's what they want, then that's the last thing I want to do. In fact, it makes me want to do even more."

Philippe let out a little laugh. "You're as stubborn as a billy goat," he said, adding, "Where are you headed from here?"

"Home." Jules swiped at his eyes with his mittened hand.

"Come on," Philippe said, standing. "I'll give you a ride."

"And my pup?" Jules asked.

"Room for the hound, too," Philippe said.

Before leaving, the two of them kicked snow over the coals. When there was nothing left but a thin trail of smoke, they stood for a moment feeling how, without the bright warmth of the fire, the night had suddenly grown so much colder and so much darker.

They walked to the edge of the hill and climbed onto the sled, Jules with the dog in his lap. Then Philippe steered it down the slope toward a distant light—the lantern Jules's mother kept burning in the window to let Jules know it was safe to come home.

WINTER CLOSES IN AGAIN

Even though Perdant had little to do with the arrests, he tried to act as if he had. He bought himself a new leather jacket and went around with his chest puffed out.

But there was no one to admire him. The town went quiet and dark. Villagers drew their curtains, turned their lamps low, and stayed inside. Or, when outside, struggled against the wind with their berets pulled over their ears and their heads tucked into their collars. It seemed as if the town had shut down.

But it had not.

Everything that went on before continued to go on, more quietly than before. Madame Desault continued to shepherd children to the plateau. Farmers continued to arrive at the station with their horse-drawn sledges and sleighs, ready to receive a child or two. Young people continued to be tucked away into boardinghouses.

Refugees managed to trickle in, as well as more and more young Frenchmen trying to avoid the compulsory labor service.

All over the plateau, shadowy figures slipped from groves of trees, crossed moonlit fields, crept into barns in darkness, joined others sleeping in haylofts. Day by day, groups of men climbed higher in the mountains, hiked farther into forests, joined other armed resisters or *maquisards*, named for the brushy terrain in which they hid and built their organization. The *maquis*—the resistance—was growing.

While all this was going on, Perdant was recording his observations, then struggling against the wind to the post office to mail thick envelopes stuffed with his reports.

As the weather closed in, the falling snow pulled a curtain between the little town and the rest of the world. Cocooned in snow, the villagers knitted sweaters, patched trousers, and stitched together plots and plans.

HENNI

At the Beehive, Henni wrote one letter to her aunt in Switzerland asking for help getting an entrance visa to that country. She hoped it was possible, even though getting an exit visa from France was probably impossible. Still, she had to try.

Then she reached for another piece of paper, intending to start a letter to Max. What should she say? What *could* she say?

With her pen poised over the paper, she thought about the last time she'd seen him—on her way back to Les Lauzes after seeing her mother deported. He'd gotten out of Gurs not long before and was staying at a Scout camp near Lyon.

Boys had been working in the garden, their voices sliced into ribbons of sound by the wind. The wind lifted swirls of dust and rocked the crowns of the trees, which cast wild shadows of light and dark on the ground. Max's white shirt billowed; his hair rippled like wheat. He adjusted his glasses, smiled his incandescent smile. Still, she could see that the trusting, happy-go-lucky fellow she'd known had been worn thin, chipped away a little.

Our youth was stolen from us, she thought, when our fathers were arrested, when we could no longer go to school, when we were called names and people spit at us, when Max had to ride his bicycle deep into the Black Forest to get away from the taunts, the jeers of "Stinking Jew!" Or when he was sent with other Jewish men to work the harvest and was paid absolutely nothing. When we were sent to the internment camp at Gurs, a place where little bites were taken out of us every day by bedbugs, lice, and fleas, and where hunger and deprivation carved away whatever dignity we still retained. And then—the deportations.

Henni told Max how she'd watched her mother and a thousand others being deported. "What will become of us?" she wondered.

Max pulled her close and said, "We'll win. When they lose—and eventually they will—we'll still be alive, and we will have won."

Max recounted the little miracles that had kept them alive so far. How he'd been released from Gurs only days before the deportations began. How, back in Germany on Kristallnacht, when the Nazi brownshirts had smashed the windows of Jewish businesses and arrested every Jewish male they could, he had quietly slipped out of town, escaping arrest.

Henni had her own miracles to recount. First of all, she had been rescued from Gurs and brought to Les Lauzes; she'd returned to the camp to visit her mother just after the lockdown. If she had arrived only the day before, she would have been locked in with everyone else.

Then, at the rail yard, how easy it would have been for her to have been scooped up with the others, locked into a cattle car, taken away . . . Yet, by a small miracle, she wasn't. Even on the train that she had taken to see

Max, when there had been a document check (she had no false papers), she had escaped—safely asleep on a pile of canvas mailbags in the mail car.

"We are still alive," Max said.

Henni rested her head on his chest, feeling it rise and fall with every breath. We might just make it, Henni thought. With luck, along with inner strength and determination, we might stay alive to see them lose.

And now, sitting at the dining table in the Beehive, she put her pen to paper and wrote, *If you're not safe there, come to Les Lauzes.*

Together they would find a way to get to safety in Switzerland.

JEAN-PAUL

There were days when Sylvie or Léon would work with Jean-Paul, stamping, cutting, trimming, gluing, stapling, and all the multitude of things that must be done to create believable documents. Céleste sometimes came, too, and sat on the sidelines, offering encouragement—convinced she would only mess things up if she tried to help. But today was not one of those days. Céleste and Sylvie were busy with school and other activities. Léon . . . Léon had been absent from school more and more until finally he just wasn't there anymore. And nobody was sure where he'd gone.

But today it suited Jean-Paul to be alone. Outside his bedroom/study/forgery office, the wind howled and raged, shaking the trees and rattling the door. Inside, dressed in three sweaters, with a hat pulled down over his ears, Jean-Paul hunched over his work, stamping, drawing, cutting, affixing.

Some days his own angry wind raged within him, angry at the injustice of it all.

But not today. Today, he was almost gleeful, even chuckling a little as he worked. Because today he was making a brand-new identity—this time for himself.

PHILIPPE

Sitting in the living area of Madame Créneau's small flat, Philippe scratched his initials into the thick frost that coated the window.

"With all that's happened, it's no longer enough to keep Jews out of sight," she said from the kitchen, where she was filling a teakettle with water. "We need to start moving people to Switzerland. Many people. And in order to do that, we need new identities for them."

From his place in the one upholstered chair, Philippe heard her set the teakettle on the stove and her footsteps as she crossed the kitchen to the door of the living room.

"Luckily, we have some good forgers," she said, appearing at the door. "We're also going to need money. And," Madame said, her sharp eyes and the knife in her hand pointed straight at him, "we are going to need guides. *Passeurs*. People smugglers."

He avoided looking directly back. Instead, he seemed to take in everything at once: The glowing embers in the wood-stove. The steaming kettle. The borders of thick frost around the edges of the windows. The quiet of the moment, as

Madame, butter knife in hand, stood perfectly still, letting her request sink in.

Because it *was* a request—Philippe was sure of that.

Not knowing what else to do, Philippe scraped his thumbnail against the frost on the window, rubbing out his initials.

"You've done well hiding people at the farms," Mme Créneau said. "You're resourceful, a quick thinker. You look younger than you are. Your survival training in Scouts, along with the uniform . . ." she continued, enumerating Philippe's qualifications.

But Philippe had stopped listening, already mapping the journey in his head. There'd be tickets to purchase, trains and buses to arrange, identity checks. No matter where you went, you'd run into German military personnel. Also, probably French border guards, maybe Italian patrols, barbed wire, dogs . . .

"Philippe?"

Philippe realized Mme Créneau was speaking to him. She stood in front of him, holding a steaming mug.

"What do you think?" she asked, handing him the tea.

He wrapped his cold hands around the hot mug and wondered if she could see his heart pulsing under his thin sweater . . . or maybe even hear it thumping.

"If you're afraid," Madame said, "that's all right. You should be. Not so afraid that you can't think straight. Just afraid enough that you stay on your toes."

Philippe blew on the tea as if to cool his enthusiasm. "Yes," he tried to say calmly, so as not to seem too eager. "I'll do it.

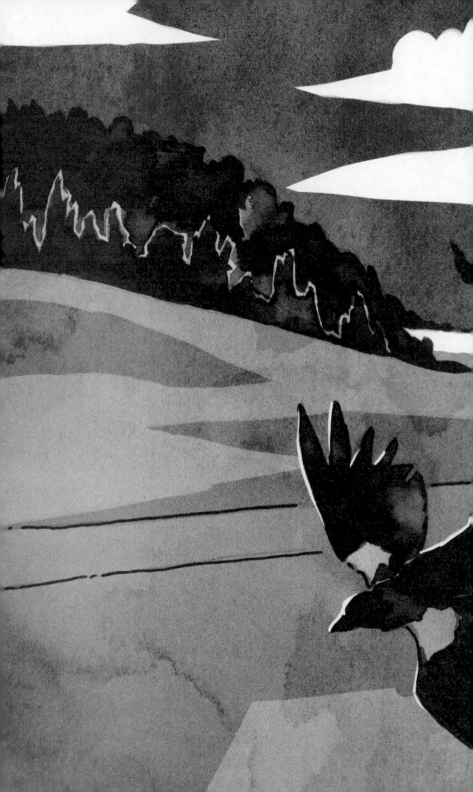

5.
SPRING 1943

A LITTLE MISSION

In March the pastors and the director of the school were released. The village breathed again, and life seemed to go back
to normal.

Little by little spring arrived, the snow melting slowly and
then all at once, creating rushing streams running down the
street to the river. *Perce-neige*, the dainty white flowers that poked
their heads out of the snow, appeared, and by late April the
hillsides quivered with broad swaths of wild yellow daffodils.

The countryside was fragrant and sometimes so quiet you
could hear a single bell on a farmer's cow clanking away or the
baaing of sheep in faraway fields. It seemed tranquil, but like
so much else, that was an illusion. Behind the sleepy facade,
things were happening. Summer residents began to trickle into
the area, along with others trying to blend in with the tourists.
Plans made in winter began to be implemented.

And on one fine May day, when the roadway was nice and
dry, Jules and Claude took a can of paint and some brushes
and did a little painting on the pavement.

JULES AND CLAUDE—CAUGHT RED-HANDED

They should have gotten away with it, but when Claude went back for the can of paint, they were caught. All the way to the policeman's office, Jules being yanked along by the arm by one German soldier and Claude prodded along by the other, Jules wondered how he might speak to Claude. He wanted to tell his friend to not mention the goats, or the lady herding the goats, or the suitcase on her back, or that she limped. But he didn't dare speak French in front of the soldiers—they'd been in France long enough to have learned some of the language—so he tried patois, the local language.

"*Ne parlez pas!*" one of the soldiers growled. "No talking!"

That ended that.

Inspector Perdant had been sitting in his office sifting through reports and complaints. There was a complaint by billeted German soldiers of clothes being stolen while they were swimming in the river. The soldiers had had to walk back to the hotel in the buff, much to the amusement of the villagers. It had turned out the clothes had not been stolen, only hidden by pranksters.

Kids. Perdant had also gotten a report that one of the local teenagers had saved a German soldier from drowning in that same river. Probably the same kid who had earlier hidden the clothes, Perdant thought.

He was shaking his head over this when German soldiers entered his office with two sheepish boys in tow.

"We have these two troublemakers caught on the road, painting," one of them said in awkward French.

"Painting . . . what?" Perdant asked, eyeing the boys.

The German either didn't want to utter the description or perhaps he didn't have enough French to manage it, so he reached over Perdant's desk, took a piece of paper and a pen, and drew a *V*—that was Churchill's victory sign—then the double-barred cross of Lorraine, the symbol of the free French army, and then *1918*, the year of Germany's defeat in World War I.

Perdant squinted at the drawing and then at the boys, wondering why. Why would they be doing something stupid like that? Something that would only draw attention to themselves when possibly their peers or family members—maybe they, themselves—were involved in the kind of illegal activity that carried the death penalty.

Generally the kids around here were careful not to do anything too stupid. And there were plenty of offenses they could have been committing but generally weren't. The interminable list included, but was not limited to: spitting at Germans, shouting "Down with Germany," wearing British or American colors, hoisting the French flag, jostling German officers, drawing caricatures of German soldiers, adopting "an anti-German attitude," and, of course, chalking, drawing, or painting forbidden symbols such as the *V* sign or the cross of Lorraine on roadways or anywhere else.

Since the Germans here were recuperating, they were not in the business of insisting the rules be enforced, but they couldn't be expected to ignore such flagrant disregard of the law.

"Your names?" he asked the boys, taking out a pad of paper and a pencil. "First and last, please."

Jules pointed at Claude and said, "Claude Dupont." He pointed at himself and said, "Jules," then hesitated, perhaps thinking better of giving his surname.

"What is your last name?" the policeman asked, his pencil poised above the paper.

Jules grumbled something that sounded to Perdant like "*La Crapule*," which meant "scoundrel." The policeman hooted. "Is that what you said? 'Scoundrel'?"

The little scoundrel gave him a scowl.

Softening his approach, Perdant asked the boy, "What does your father do?"

"He is a prisoner of war," Jules said.

"Ah," Perdant said gently.

Jules solemnly bowed his head.

The little one, the "scoundrel," was only ten or eleven years old, but Perdant suspected he knew far more than he let on. The other, bigger boy looked like a simpleton, a dullard, with heavy brows and heavy eyelids, his mouth hanging open as they sat awaiting their fate. The little one had bright eyes and, Perdant sensed, a kind of canny intelligence. The ringleader, Perdant assumed.

He drummed his pencil on his desk and stared at the boys. Why take the time to paint all three symbols? It was almost as if they were *trying* to take as long as they possibly could.

The most likely explanation was that it had been a diversionary tactic. Someone of more consequence had escaped into the woods or contraband had been disposed of while the Germans concentrated on catching these two delinquents.

But he could hardly scold the soldiers for being idiots, and he supposed it was his duty to take it seriously—even more so when an officer walked through the door.

After being filled in by the soldiers, the officer let his gaze travel over the boys, pausing for a moment to give Claude a look of disgust. "I hope you intend to punish these troublemakers appropriately," the man said, turning away from the boys toward Perdant.

"Look," Perdant said. "They're just kids being kids. I doubt they even know what those symbols mean."

The officer gave him a sour look.

"All right," Perdant said. "They probably do. Still, they're just kids."

"What is it you *do*, by the way?" the officer asked, gazing all about the room as if looking for an indication of the young man's position.

Perdant did not think that question really required a reply, but as he was speaking to an officer, he answered, "I am a police inspector."

The officer looked him up and down and shook his head. "Are the French accustomed to having teenagers serve in the police force?"

"I am almost twenty-three," Perdant said. He would have liked to point out that some of the German soldiers billeted in the hotel were barely old enough to shave, but he kept his mouth shut on the subject.

The officer continued to shake his head while pacing the room, pausing to peer closely at Perdant's framed diploma. "Well, that explains the lack of attention to matters in this town, I suppose."

"Excuse me?" Perdant said.

"It is rumored that the village is a nest of deserters, communists, Jews, and other undesirables," the officer said. "Yet here you are, advocating leniency toward two miscreants brought in by alert German troops."

Perdant had an opinion as to how alert the soldiers had been, but he kept it to himself.

"We have heard reports that there are hundreds of Jews hiding here—all over in this area." The officer made a big, stiff circle with his arm. "If you are not going to take matters in hand, perhaps *we* will have to do it."

The officer swept out the door before Perdant could respond. The two soldiers scurried after him without a backward glance.

Perdant's face stung as if slapped. Why was he continually made to feel like a fool? He stood for a moment looking at the door by which they had exited, feeling a mix of embarrassment and remorse. And something else. Dread.

He was about to go out and try to clear his head with a walk in the fresh air when he remembered the boys. He cleared his throat and crossed the room to where they were seated, then took a moment to set a chair backward in front of the boys and straddle it.

"Now," he said, resting his arms on the back of the chair, "tell me what you were doing out on that road when those soldiers nabbed you."

The younger one, Jules, obviously accustomed to doing the talking, chimed in and said, "Just messing around. I guess it was stupid. We're sorry."

"Yes, of course it was stupid," Perdant said. "But more than that, it's a punishable offense."

Jules nodded and looked at his hands, as if surprised to see them sitting idly on his lap.

"Who or what were you protecting?"

Jules looked up and said, "Protecting?" in a way that sounded so innocent, Perdant knew it couldn't be.

The other boy's expression did not change. Just as dull as always. Still, it was worth a shot, Perdant thought. He turned to Claude.

"Was there someone important you were protecting by distracting the soldiers?" he asked Claude.

Claude's eyes flickered with confusion.

"I don't think he understands all those big words," Jules whispered.

"Who got away when you were painting on the road?" Perdant asked the older boy.

Claude's eyes widened. The corners of his mouth turned up slightly. "American lady," he said.

Perdant wrote that down.

Claude went on talking in a kind of disjointed way, while Perdant scribbled down the words he could make out in the boy's garbled speech. "Bicycle radio. Wooden leg. Old château. Spy lady."

"The American lady is the spy?" Perdant asked, somewhat incredulously.

He noticed Jules shaking his head, so he turned to the younger boy.

Jules rolled his eyes and said, "I think he's talking about a movie he saw in Le Puy."

Come to think of it, Perdant thought he'd seen that same movie. "Fine. *You* can go," he said to Claude. "But don't let me ever catch you painting those signs on the road or anywhere else—do you understand?"

Claude looked at Jules, who nodded, so he got up and went toward the door. Jules started to follow.

"*You*," Perdant said. "Not so fast."

Jules turned back, and Claude hesitated.

"Clo-clo, you go home, okay?" Jules said.

"Now?"

"Yeah."

Claude went out, and Jules returned to his seat, his face a mask.

"You know I could send you to jail," Perdant said.

The boy's face didn't change. They must give classes in this stuff here, Perdant thought. "But I'll tell you what. If you'd like to help me out a little, I'll let you off the hook. How about that?"

"What kind of help?" asked the boy.

"For now just keep an eye out. Maybe run a few errands for me." When the little scoundrel didn't immediately respond, he added, "Report to me what you see. Any little detail. Any little item of interest."

"I don't know," the boy said. "I'm very busy."

"It's not an option!" Perdant said, growing frustrated. "I'm giving you an opportunity so you don't have to go to jail."

"Oh," said Jules.

"Listen," Perdant said more gently. "I'll tell you what. If you help me out, I'll do what I can to get your father released from prison. I might be able to pull a few strings."

The boy nodded slightly, so Perdant went on. "Report to me every Tuesday and Thursday from now on. Nine o'clock in the morning."

Jules started to protest until Perdant turned a glacial blue eye on him and shut him down.

"*Oui, Monsieur*," Jules said.

Once the boy was out of the office, Perdant put away his reports and, reaching for the telephone, turned his attention to bigger things.

THE RAID

In the past when there'd been raids, there'd been a phone call the night before.

"How's the weather up there?" someone from the police station in the valley would ask. Or a quick, "*Fais attention!*—Watch out!" Then the line would go dead—hung up on the other end. Just enough to know that precautions should be taken.

But there was no warning one early spring morning when a dozen police trucks and motorcycles wound up the mountain and burst upon the slumbering village and surrounding countryside.

People woke to the rumble of cars and motorcycles and the low, throbbing idling of a bus, a bus that had been brought along to cart away all those they planned to arrest.

At the Beehive, Henni and the others were awakened by pounding at the door. They heard Monsieur Boulet go to the door and, sitting in their beds, barely breathing, caught snatches of the conversation.

"Can I help you?" That was M. Boulet.

"We've come for any non-Aryans. They are to be transferred elsewhere." That was the standard line, delivered by a standard policeman.

Henni and the others could not see the policemen; they could only hear the shuffling of their boots, their rough voices, and feel the weight of their presence.

"This house is under the protection of the Swiss government," M. Boulet was telling them. "And these children are under my protection. You'll have to produce a warrant if you want to search here."

"To get a warrant we'll have to go all the way back to Le Puy," whined a voice on the far side of the door.

"So, go back to Le Puy," said M. Boulet. "I won't let you enter without the proper authorization."

There was more discussion, frustrated mumbling, and at last the clatter of boots down the walk, multiple car doors slamming, and the sound of the cars driving away.

The young children sat in their beds, wide-eyed. The older ones who had crept to the stairs to listen now stared at one another in disbelief. Had the policemen really left to drive all the way back to Le Puy? *All* of them?

"Breakfast!" M. Boulet called up the stairs, and everyone sprang to action.

»»«

It is happening, Henni thought as she shoveled oatmeal into her mouth, then a spoonful into little Lulu's. Her face felt numb. The oatmeal made a heavy lump in her stomach.

"Blueberry-picking day!" M. Boulet called out, handing the children baskets.

"Blueberries . . . ?" Henni asked him incredulously. It was only May.

"I mean, mushroom hunting!" he exclaimed, then whispered to her, "Henni, you will keep an eye on the little ones, won't you? If they find any mushrooms, don't let them eat any until they can be checked by the pharmacist."

Henni nodded as he handed her Lulu, at only three years old, the youngest.

"Someone will let you know when it's safe to return" was the last thing he said as she led the children out the back door and toward the forest.

THE SEARCH BEGINS;
ARRESTS ARE MADE

"Leave no stone unturned," Perdant told the gendarmes before they set off in all directions. "Search attics, cellars. Open closets, cupboards, drawers. Knock on walls for secret panels. Check floors for trapdoors. Look everywhere."

He pictured the gendarmes and policemen fanning out across the town and countryside like a huge net, scooping up big silvery fish and little minnows: foreigners, suspects, black marketers, and Jews.

It was a delicate matter, this business of Jew catching. There were French Jews and foreign Jews. There were registered or unregistered Jews. Documented and undocumented. There were some living in houses supposedly under the protection of the Swiss government. But what a lot of the people sheltering these enemies of the nation didn't seem to understand was that the laws and regulations about who was legal and who was not had changed. And now, if they were sheltering Jews, they themselves could—and needed to know they *would*—be arrested.

As for Perdant, he, too, had arrests to make. His first stop was the carpentry workshop.

>> <<

"Aha! Now I've got you!" Perdant said as he burst into the woodworking shop. It had seemed very dramatic when he'd practiced it in the mirror the day before, but when he saw the puzzled looks on the two boys' faces, he realized how ridiculous it sounded. Still, in addition to confusion, there was fear on those faces, and that was a more satisfying reaction.

The two brothers were put on the bus to wait for all the non-Aryans and undesirables that Perdant was certain would soon be coming.

In the meantime, local children and teens were arriving with little gifts for the boys; they'd begun to surround the bus and started singing. But Perdant had another arrest to make and needed to go. Leaving a few gendarmes to guard the brothers, he went off with the sound of young voices in his ears.

IN THE WOODS

How far is far enough? Henni wondered as she led her young charges into the woods. Her friend Madeleine walked alongside her. Madeleine was just as old as Henni, but somehow Henni seemed to be the one in charge.

The littlest of the children, two boys and one girl, skipped and jumped, squealing and giggling.

"Quietly!" Henni gently scolded. Instantly, the children stopped chattering, held hands, and walked nearly silently along the path.

Henni smiled sadly at their spindly legs, bare below their shorts and skirt. It was one thing to be in your teens and live through all this. She, at least, could remember better times. These little tykes probably couldn't remember a time when . . . *Well, never mind,* she told herself, shaking memories of her old life out of her head. Maybe it was better not to remember.

It was, she told herself, a beautiful day to be in the forest, and she tried to think about how the light filtering through the branches made little squares of sunlight on the path ahead. The children had already forgotten about being quiet and had resumed leaping from one bright spot to the next, letting out little squeaks of delight. Henni didn't have the heart to stop them.

How far? she wondered again. How far was far enough? Would the police trouble themselves to go hunting in the woods? What if they had dogs?

Henni peered into the forest, looking for large boulders or thickly growing trees. Where did you go to hide from dogs?

Back home in Germany, she had seen the storm trooper's big brown-and-black dogs straining against their leashes, their teeth bared, their black eyes glittering. All that had separated her from them were the thin leather leashes held by sneering soldiers. The song she'd heard the soldiers sing as they marched below her bedroom window haunted her. "When Jewish blood spurts from the knife, then things go twice as well . . ."

Her blood seemed to freeze at the memory of it, as if it were refusing to run through her veins or anywhere at all.

She felt a small hand tugging on her skirt. "Where are the mushrooms, Henni?" Lulu asked, looking up at her.

"A little farther." Henni strained to hear what might be happening in the town behind them while leading the children deeper into the forest.

"I'm hungry!" Pepi piped up.

"But we can't eat any mushrooms," Henni said. "You can pick but not eat."

"What will we *eat*?" Pepi cried.

"Maybe we'll find some blueberries," Henni said, knowing they would not.

She tried to listen with her whole being for the roar of motorcycles or trucks on the road or barking dogs or policemen crashing through the woods. But all that could be heard were the peaceful sounds of the forest: the wind pushing the tops of the pines, the flutter of birds among the bushes, the complaint of a crow somewhere distant.

Lulu tripped over a root, fell and scraped her knee on a rock, and started howling, her shrieks echoing through the forest. The two boys, Simon and Pepi, had gotten into a tussle, and now Simon was crying as well. And Pepi was whining, "I'm hungreee!"

"If you will all promise to be quiet, I will tell you a story," Henni said.

"Tell us a story!" Lulu said through her tears.

"Can you stop crying?" Henni asked.

Lulu nodded, sniffling.

"Simon?"

Simon wiped his nose on his sleeve and nodded, too.

"Well, then," Henni said, walking as she talked. "Once upon a time there was . . ." And then she realized only one story came to mind. She paused. Could she really not think of a single other story?

"Once upon a time what?" Pepi said.

Madeleine rolled her eyes. "Are you going to tell the story or what?" she said.

"*You* think of a story," Henni said to her friend.

"I don't know any stories," Madeleine pronounced.

Henni sighed and went on, thinking, Well, here goes. "Once upon a time," she said, "a poor woodcutter lived in the forest with his two children, Hansel and Gretel. His new wife, the children's stepmother, said to the father, 'There is not enough food for us in this house. You must get rid of the children. Take them out into the woods—take them deep, deep into the forest so they will never find their way back.'"

Henni noticed the children were completely silent now. Simon and Pepi walked with their heads down, staring at the ground. This was probably a very bad tale to have chosen, she realized. But at least they were quiet. She peered into the forest and wondered again how far they should go.

A CUP OF COFFEE

Was that a curtain being pulled aside? Perdant wondered as he looked up at the windows of the residence. He was about to step back to get a better view when the door opened and he was greeted by a stout woman in a white apron.

"Can I help you?" she said, pointing the spoon in her hand at him—as if there might be some confusion as to which "you" she was addressing.

"I wish to speak with . . ." He consulted his notebook unnecessarily. He knew the fellow's name, but he liked to give the impression of having so many names in his book that he had to consult it each time. "Anton Smelyansky," he said.

She gestured for him to enter, and he followed her into the house and down a hall lined with unfortunately closed doors. He would have liked to take a look into those rooms.

"Please sit down and have a cup of coffee," the woman said when they came to the kitchen. "I'll go find him."

"No thank you," Perdant said. "I'll just—"

"Nonsense!" she said. "It will only take a minute." The cook slid a plate with a thick slice of bread toward him. She plunked a jar of jam onto the table and nodded at it. "Would you open that? Arthritis," she explained, holding up her hands as evidence.

Perdant loosened the lid and lifted it off. Immediately, he got a noseful of *summer*. In spite of himself, he began to salivate.

"Help yourself!" the cook said, gesturing to a pot of creamy butter and the glistening red jam, lumpy with raspberries. "Sit down! Sit down!" she insisted. "Coffee's almost ready." She pulled out a chair, gestured to it, and croaked, "Ha! If you can call roasted chickory or ground-up acorns coffee!"

In spite of his plan not to, he began spreading butter on the bread. And after the butter, jam. He caught a glimpse of a little head peeking in through the kitchen door.

"Now, who was it you wanted to see?" the cook asked.

Perdant looked at his notebook as if he needed to remind himself. Of course he did not. He had practiced in his room before arriving. But it seemed he hadn't rehearsed what would happen if he were offered a cup of coffee. "Anton Smelyan-sky," he said with his mouth embarrassingly full. "If I might just . . ." He turned toward the door—the little head was gone.

Were those footsteps he heard overhead? Possibly scurrying footsteps? It was hard to hear over the running water and the coffeepot boiling on the stove, and now the cook's clomping *sabots*.

A steaming mug of ersatz coffee was set in front of him— Perdant had a dizzying sense that hours had passed or no time at all. He'd noticed this before, the way the passage of time seemed skewed. It was one of the odd things about this village.

There were other strange things. Sometimes he heard a weird metallic jingling like that of spurs. But when he looked, there was never anything there.

Perdant tapped a knife against the oilcloth on the table, trying not to think about the time he was wasting. He listened to the sound of kids running in and out, footsteps on the stairs, going up, coming down. He stared out the kitchen window at the forest that swept down from the mountainsides and crept right into the backyards of these homes—vast, dark ribbons of pines laced with deer and rabbit trails, and filled with ferns big enough to conceal small children.

THE STORY

"The story, Henni!" Lulu urged. She held up her arms to be carried.

Henni bent down so the little girl could climb onto her back, then carried her piggyback while she went on with the story.

"Hansel," she said, "had overheard the conversation between his father and his stepmother and had put a crust of bread in his pocket. He had a plan. The next day the father took them far into the forest. Gretel was frightened and cried, but Hansel was very brave, like all of you. He kept his wits. All along the way, he left a little trail of bread crumbs to follow so that he and his sister might find their way home."

Henni adjusted Lulu on her back as she thought about the next part of the story. Was it too sad for the little ones? But the children were quiet, waiting for the story to go on, so she continued. "'I'm frightened!' Gretel cried. 'I'm cold and hungry and I want to go home!'

"'Don't be afraid,' Hansel said. 'I've left a trail of bread crumbs we can follow.'"

Henni stopped, noticing that they had come to a beautiful open area filled with blueberry bushes, covered, not with blueberries, but with tiny green buds.

"Look!" Henni said. "Blueberry bushes!"

"Are these *all* blueberry bushes?" Pepi asked.

"Yes," Henni answered. "See if you can find any berries."

The children crawled among the bushes, and Henni plunked herself down, too. Had they gone far enough? She didn't know.

She wished Max were there, then stopped wishing that and just hoped he was safe—wherever he was. *Max*, she thought wistfully, settling herself among the bushes, *where are you now?*

Absently plucking at the leaves of a blueberry bush, she laughed a little to think of falling in love in a concentration camp—where you shivered on your hard plank bunk or the even harder floor of a barracks filled to bursting with starving women and girls, where the first thing every morning was a gruff man sticking his head in the door and shouting, "Got any?" Meaning, dead. And often there were . . .

"I'm hungree!" Pepi cried. "And I can't find any blueberries!"

"Keep telling the story, Henni!" Simon said. "We can listen while we look for berries."

"Stay close then, so I can speak quietly," Henni said.

Lulu came and climbed onto Henni's lap, stuck her thumb in her mouth, and gazed up into the older girl's face. The others gave up on their futile hunt for berries and clustered around Henni, looking at her expectantly.

"Well," said Henni, "remember that Hansel had left a trail of bread crumbs. But when he and Gretel went to look, they couldn't find the crumbs. Hungry birds had eaten them all. There was no trail left."

Pepi and Simon looked at Henni, their faces grave. Young as they were, they already had little furrows between their eyebrows when they frowned.

"What did they do?" Simon whispered.

"Did they have anything to eat?" Pepi asked.

"They did not have anything to eat," Henni said. "And they looked and looked for the bread crumb trail, but soon realized that they were well and truly lost."

Henni paused again and listened. All she heard was Lulu, earnestly sucking her thumb.

"On they walked until they came to a beautiful glade." Henni gestured around her. "Like this one. Except there was a little cottage in it, and it was made of bread. The roof was made of cake, and the windows were made of clear sugar."

Lulu pulled her thumb out of her mouth and said breathlessly, "And chocolate?"

"Yes, chocolate!" Henni said. "And peppermints and hard candies and sweets of all sorts stuck all over the cottage. Of course Hansel and Gretel were starving, so they began to stuff themselves with all these delicious things.

"'Nibble, nibble, little mouse!' came a voice." Henni made her voice as scratchy as an old crone's. "'Who's that nibbling at my house?'"

"Was it a witch?" Simon asked.

"It *was* a witch," Henni said. "But Hansel and Gretel didn't know that, and at first the witch acted nice and told them to come inside, and she fed them milk and pancakes with sugar, apples, and nuts. The children thought they were in heaven. But not for long, for soon she threw Hansel into a cage! She wanted to fatten him up before she ate him!

"But here is the thing about witches," Henni went on. "They have a sense of smell like dogs do and can always tell when humans are near. But they have very poor eyesight. So when the witch went every day to check to see if Hansel was getting fatter, he stuck a chicken bone between the bars, and the witch felt the skinny bone instead. In this way, he put off getting eaten.

"But one day, skinny or not, she decided it was time to eat Hansel, and maybe Gretel as well. So she made a big fire in the oven. Then she told Gretel, 'Climb in and see if the oven is hot enough.'

"Gretel saw what the old witch had in mind. She did not want to climb inside the oven, so she said, 'I don't know how to do that. How can I get inside?'

"'Stupid goose!' said the witch. 'The opening is big enough even for me—see?' and she swung the door of the oven open to show Gretel.

"Then Gretel gave her a shove, and the mean old witch went right inside and burned up! And that was the end of that old witch!"

Henni stopped, hoping they would accept that as the end of the story. She didn't want to go on.

Lulu mumbled around her thumb, "Why did the witch want to eat Hansel? Why didn't she eat her own house that was made of candy?"

"She hated children," Pepi said.

"She was just bad and mean," Simon said.

Henni listened to them, noticing the first bright little insects of spring fluttering in the sunbeams.

"Why are some people bad and some people good?" Lulu asked.

"I don't know," Henni said. She wished she knew. She wished she could tell the children, explain the world, but she didn't understand anything about it.

"I'm going to be good," Lulu said. "Like Monsieur Boulet."

"Like Madame Desault," said Madeleine.

"Like you, Henni," said Pepi.

Henni felt tears spring to her eyes. She pressed her lips together. She did not want to cry. Not here! Not now!

"Why is it bad to be Jewish?" Pepi asked.

Again, Henni couldn't answer. She herself had often felt ashamed of it, though she was old enough to know there was no reason to.

"But not here," said Simon. "Here it is all right."

The others nodded, agreeing.

"Then what happened, Henni? Tell the rest of the story!" Pepi said, bouncing on his knees in front of her.

"Shh," said Madeleine, suddenly alert and listening.

"What?" Henni said.

Madeleine held up her hand and tilted her head toward town.

Everyone held their breath and kept perfectly still, even little Lulu. And then they all heard it.

The sound of young voices singing, "*Au claire de la lune, mon ami, Pierrot . . .*" Their housemates who had not had to hide were singing to let them know it was safe to come back.

"I'm hungreeee . . ." Pepi cried, running toward them. The others were already up and starting down the path toward the voices.

Henni rose and took Lulu's hand. She was so weary. Weary with relief that the long day was coming to an end. And weary with relief that she hadn't had to tell the end of the story, when Hansel and Gretel go home to their waiting, loving father. Henni knew that she and most of the other children would never see their fathers again.

Henni sang along with the voices coming up the forest path. *"Ouvre-moi ta porte, pour l'amour de Dieu,"* she sang. "Open your door to me, for the love of God."

6.

**LATE MAY 1943
IN THE FOREST
OUTSIDE LES LAUZES**

THE MAGIC CIRCLE

There was, Max thought, something magical about this place, just as Henni had suggested. Branches curved over him and the still-sleeping form of his companion like the arches of a cathedral, or the vaulted ceiling of a mosque, or the graceful curving eaves of a temple. That was the nice thing about forests, he thought, they didn't subscribe to any one religion or ideology. A forest was as accepting of one person sleeping in it as another, no matter who you were or what you believed.

Perhaps it was this that made the forest seem magical, or maybe it was the way the sunlight filtered through the pine boughs, making lacy patterns on his rumpled shirt, across the forest floor, and over the face of his still-sleeping friend.

The boy let out little puffs of air as he slept, and Max tried dropping bits of catkin fluff over his mouth at the precise moment of his exhalations, to see if his breath would lift the fuzz into the air. Instead, a bit of it ended up in the boy's mouth, and he awoke, spitting.

"Something must be falling from the trees," Max explained.

"Hmm," said his friend, sounding unconvinced.

"I wonder what time it is." Max squinted up at the sun glimmering through the tops of the trees.

"And what that sound is," Max's friend said.

Max heard it, too: a kind of distant creaking rattle coming toward them.

"I hope this place is as safe as Henni said it is," Max said. "Even though she said there's a policeman in town now." Had that policeman received word about Max and his friend from the station in Lyon, where the police were actively looking for them? There was no way to know.

They had hiked their way up to the plateau, walking at night and sleeping in forests during the day. They'd arrived on the outskirts of Les Lauzes in the middle of the night, and Max had been stymied. Just how did he think he would find Henni?

Now there were voices. Girls' voices.

The rattling, it soon became apparent, came from a wooden cart being pulled along the path by a couple of teenage girls. One of those girls—shoulders back, face forward, wearing a little crown of sunshine on her fair hair—looked just like Henni. Was he really seeing her, Max wondered, or had he conjured her out of the morning mist still lingering in the forest? Maybe this was a moment like others he'd experienced when—even though he knew she was miles away—it seemed as if she were right there with him.

"Is that someone you know?" his companion whispered, seeing Max staring, transfixed. The girls were past them now, moving away.

Max nodded and stood up, knowing then that the Henni he saw was not an apparition.

"Shall we call to them?" his friend asked, getting up.

"Wait," Max said, trying to smooth the wrinkles out of his shirt. "She'll think this is funny," he said, and put his fingers to his lips.

≫ ≪

Henni and her friend had taken the path through the woods to get to a farm where they would pick up food for the Beehive. While Madeleine chattered away, Henni thought of Max, wondering where he was and hoping he was safe. She'd told him to come to Les Lauzes, but that was before the raids. Maybe, she thought, it wasn't so safe here anymore. Ever since she and the children had had to hide in these woods, her heart beat a little faster whenever she walked through them. The tall, straight trees, standing in tidy rows like ranks of soldiers, unnerved her. She felt as if helmeted German soldiers hid behind the mossy green trunks. So, at first, when she heard the wolf whistle, every nerve end bristled.

Then she thought, Stupid boys from school.

Madeleine turned around to look, and Henni said, "Don't turn around. It's just boys from school being obnoxious."

"I don't know . . ." Madeleine said, turning back to Henni. "Maybe you should turn around."

"No!" Henni said. "Don't encourage whoever it is."

"I really think you should look," Madeleine urged.

Henni turned slowly to see Max grinning at her, his bright eyes managing to shine through the smudgy lenses of his glasses, which teetered a little lopsided on his face. His face was lit with a smile as if he had just happened on the best moment of his life.

THE SOLICITATION

Céleste was hunting for asparagus in the overgrown grass along one of the stone walls outside of town when Jules's head popped up from behind the wall. She was so startled she dropped both the asparagus and the knife she'd been using to cut it.

"Jules!" she said.

"Shh!" he hissed, scanning the roadway behind her. "Any sign of Perdant? He's trying to get me to spy for him."

She looked over her shoulder. "No," she said. "Are you in trouble?"

"Not yet." He climbed over the wall to where she stood. "Or, well, maybe. I don't want to find out."

"How do you do that, anyway," Céleste asked, "popping up out of nowhere like that?"

"It's my superpower," Jules said. "I'm like Superman!"

"Who?" Céleste muttered, now on her hands and knees hunting for the knife and the thin asparagus stalks—nearly invisible in the tall green grass.

"Superman! The man of steel? Faster than a speeding bullet?" Jules said.

"Never heard of him."

"He's American. In a comic book. He always shows up when people need his help."

"Well, Superman, I could use some help finding the asparagus you made me lose."

Jules dropped down into the grass and began scurrying around on his knees.

"Be careful!" Céleste admonished. "There's a knife, too— and the blade is open! But maybe that doesn't matter if you're—what did you say—a man of steel?"

Jules's hand appeared above the grass, waving several stalks of sandy asparagus. "This it?" he said.

Céleste took the precious stalks, stood, and tucked them into her skirt pocket.

Still on his hands and knees, Jules said, "I have a message for you. Someone wants to meet you at the Château de Roque. Alone. You're supposed to go alone."

"That place?" Céleste said. "It's been empty forever."

"Yeah, that place," Jules said.

"Well, who? Who wants to meet me there?"

"I'm not supposed to say."

"Are you hiding down there or are you looking for my knife?" Céleste said.

"Both," Jules said.

"I'm not going to go to a creepy old abandoned château all by myself if I don't even know who I'm supposed to meet!" Céleste cried.

Jules's finger emerged from above the grass, beckoning her to crouch down near him. When she did, he whispered, "It's Léon."

Well, well, Céleste thought. Léon.

"And here's your knife," Jules said, handing her the knife, its blade safely tucked away in its wooden handle.

Then, as quickly as he'd appeared, he was gone again.

➤➤◄◄

Later, Céleste wheeled her bike up the drive to the château. It was really just a path now, the drive overgrown with long grass and wildflowers. Ahead, there was a grove of sadly neglected fruit trees, a garden taken over by Scotch broom, and the imposing, castle-like house, its wooden shutters hanging from their hinges. Its turret was covered in old vines, its majestic front steps covered with moss and wild violets.

She'd heard there'd been heartbreak here: a young man killed in a long-ago war. The parents' hearts broken, the young wife moved away. Nothing to show that children had ever lived here. No diapers hanging on a clothesline, no little bicycle or pram parked outside the door. She realized now that at every other farm on the plateau, what you saw was evidence of children. Perhaps, Céleste thought, it is all these children everywhere—never out of our sight—that keep compassion intact, the path clear.

She propped her bike against the stone wall, then pushed open the creaking gate.

Léon appeared from the orchard. His clothes were rumpled and a bit battered, and his face sunbrowned, even though winter was barely over. Was that a bit of a beard on his chin? Then she saw the pistol at his side and realized—

"You've joined the *maquis*!" she cried. "Why? You're too young!"

"There are plenty of boys younger than me here," he said, pointing his barely bearded chin toward the woods beyond.

This made Céleste immeasurably sad and tired. She felt like an old grandmother whose grandchildren had gone to war. "But you were doing good work in Les Lauzes. Why isn't that enough?"

"The time has come to really serve my country. It's happening soon, Céleste, the liberation!" He clutched her shoulders, his eyes bright with optimism—or something—fatigue, maybe; Céleste couldn't tell.

"Germany's been beaten back at the Eastern Front. The Allies have taken Tunisia. Next they'll move into Italy. From Italy to France, Céleste. I want to be part of the liberation. I want to help make it happen."

"I'm so afraid for you," Céleste said.

"Don't be afraid." Léon looked into her eyes. "This is what I want to do. It feels right."

Céleste pressed her lips together to keep herself silent.

"We all must do everything we can, don't you agree?" Léon said.

Céleste hesitated before she said yes.

"Would you be willing to do something for us?"

"Why don't you ask Sylvie?" Céleste asked. "Is it because she's your sister, so you don't want to put her in danger?"

"She doesn't approve of what we're doing. She believes

we should continue with nonviolent methods, like our pastors advocate."

"Well, what makes you think I don't agree with her?"

"I think you want to do something to help. I think you always have. I'm just giving you the opportunity. I'm not going to argue with you about the right or wrong of armed resistance. I know Pastor Autin advocates using only 'weapons of the spirit' in our fight against the Nazis, but those kinds of weapons only go so far."

"Do they?" Céleste challenged him. "Guns and tanks will rust, break, and eventually turn to dust. But the spirit prevails."

"Nice thought, but I just don't believe the spirit alone will prevail against the Wehrmacht. In this case we have to fight firepower with firepower. Don't worry, I'm not asking you to carry or fire a gun; I'm not asking you to kill anyone. It's only to carry a little message. Can you do it? *Will* you do it?"

All the way back to town, Céleste rode slowly along the path through the forest, barely noticing the spattering of sunlight on the ferns, the fluttering of a white moth, a purple butterfly. She'd have to give Léon an answer soon, but she needed time to think about it.

It was true that she had long wanted to do something, but now at the thought of it her heart drummed mercilessly inside her chest—so hard she could barely pedal her bicycle. She was too frightened. She would mess up. Something would go wrong. She'd always imagined that she would get involved in dangerous work someday, but that was imagining herself as some other person—someone more like Sylvie: confident, strong, a little bigger maybe, someone *brave*. She'd never been any of those things. And she still wasn't.

She turned into the forest, so deep in thought that she hardly noticed the roots and stones over which the bicycle bounced.

Just ahead of her, two girls stepped onto the path, and Céleste lurched to a stop. "Henni!" she squeaked. "Madeleine! What—?" She cut her question short when she noticed the two young men standing in the forest not far away.

Henni breathlessly rushed through an explanation, ending with the plea, "Can you help us?"

Céleste almost couldn't answer, she was struck so forcefully with a kind of realization—something that should have been obvious, but somehow she had not really understood it in the depths of her heart until this moment. Some people, she realized, were having a very different experience than her own. While she had been fretting over whether she was too fearful to do this or that, people like Henni and the young men she wanted to help lived in fear every single moment. They had no choice but to be brave. They had no choice but to take action.

Why had she never stopped to think what it would be like to be Henni—or any of the other Jewish teens and children scattered in farms and houses all over the plateau, separated from their families, not knowing where their parents were or if they were still alive, having to hide when neighbors stopped by, never knowing what would happen next? Why did she think she should be so privileged to escape being afraid now and then?

"Yes, of course I'll help," she said, knowing now that she would also help Léon.

7.

JUNE 1943

LE PASSEUR–
THE PEOPLE SMUGGLER

As usual, Philippe arrived at the safe house dressed in his Scout uniform: shorts, shirt with badges affixed, beret, and scarf. There, he was introduced to his "travelers." By now he'd made a number of these journeys. Through the late winter into spring, and finally summer.

This time his travelers were a couple whom Philippe knew only as Armand and his wife, Lucile. Armand was French; Lucile, German. Armand had been wounded in World War I; he'd had a business in Paris. Lucile was a nurse. According to their new identification papers, they were French, from Alsace. It was imperative that Lucile not speak, as her heavily German-accented French would fool no one.

Philippe took note of—and approved—their nondescript clothes and decent walking shoes. They carried very little in the way of luggage. All to the good—there would be less to convince them to leave behind once they reached their final stop.

He also knew by now they would have been filled in on the "rules" of travel that Madame Créneau would have recited:

You are hereby warned that the trip involves risks and there is no guarantee for anybody. If you agree, good luck!

A young man will come looking for you at this house. Follow him at a distance.

So far, so good, he thought, walking in the direction of the train station. The couple followed at a distance as they had been instructed to do at all times.

Just before you depart, the young man will give you your train tickets. If someone asks for your ticket or your proof of identity, act as though nothing important has happened and you aren't bothered. Don't speak.

The beginning of the trip was the easy part. As he would for every segment of the journey, Philippe bought and then gave the tickets to the travelers as unobtrusively as possible before they boarded. The couple would sit separately from him, and they and Philippe would pretend not to know each other.

Philippe's rule, when involved in an action, was to stay focused. Buying tickets, getting the tickets to the refugees, boarding the train, taking a seat, having identity cards checked: Stay alert. Keep your eyes and ears open. Listen. Watch. Observe. Think only about that moment. The time to review the next steps was on the long rides or waiting for the next connection.

This leg of the trip had gone off without a hitch. He and the travelers disembarked and only had to wait for their next train. Now was a time to think through the future steps.

This was what he was doing while leaning on a pillar in the station at Dunières when he noticed someone who looked like Céleste. The fashionable skirt, that blouse, the dark curls framing her heart-shaped face, the way she tucked her hair behind her ear . . . It *was* Céleste! He felt a rush of . . . what? Something like the adrenaline rush he sometimes got when the German police approached or something looked dicey. It was sort of like that—his heart lurching wildly—and it surprised him. He saw her all the time in Les Lauzes and his heart didn't do acrobatic stunts then . . . Did it?

He'd taken a few steps toward her before he realized what he was doing and stopped. *No distractions*, he reminded himself. The last thing he needed was to miss a train connection or lose track of his travelers. For another, she looked . . . Well, he had the distinct impression that she'd seen him and was pretending that she hadn't. Why? Where was she going? With a suitcase?

Philippe had the urge to speak to her, but he reminded himself he needed to keep his attention on his travelers. It would be unconscionable if they missed the train to Saint-Étienne because he'd been chatting with a friend. While he considered all this, Céleste disappeared in the swirl of people.

Sitting on the next train, and on the long walk to the Revols' house, Armand and Lucile trailing behind, Philippe wondered about that chance encounter. Where was Céleste going? Her family lived in Paris. But she wasn't headed toward the Paris-bound trains. She had been headed in the other direction.

These thoughts dogged him all the way to the Revols' farm. There, Armand and Lucile were ensconced in the barn and offered stew made with vegetables from the garden, along with some bread and a portion of cheese.

Philippe sat with a bowl of the same stew at the kitchen table while Madame Revol rinsed strawberries from their garden under the tap and spoke about the roundups in Lyon and the destruction of old Marseille.

"They're starting to get desperate, the *boches*," she said. "And they are getting meaner."

Philippe tried to keep his mind on the conversation, but his thoughts drifted to the moment he'd seen Céleste. Was it possible it wasn't Céleste, but just someone who looked like her? No. The more he thought about it, the more certain he was that it had been her.

Mme Revol set a bowl of still-wet strawberries—tiny beads of water shimmering on their surface—on the table. Philippe stared at them as if at a bowl of diamond-encrusted rubies.

"They're also saying," she murmured, "that Lyon is crawling with the men in leather jackets and felt hats."

"Plainclothes German police," Philippe said. It was no secret that they favored leather jackets and felt hats. He also knew there would be a long wait in Lyon for the train to Annecy. He bit into a strawberry, tasting the sweetness of the fruit, followed by a slight bitter aftertaste of fear. "We arrive in Lyon at six thirty or seven o'clock and leave at midnight, so there's quite a wait," he acknowledged, "but I'm sure it will go fine. This couple has been doing everything right. They're conscientious, thoughtful, intelligent. They haven't made any missteps."

"Good," Mme Revol said. Her gaze fell to the strawberry she was slicing into a bowl.

Philippe's mind flitted again to the sight of Céleste walking away. She hadn't looked like her normal, sassy, playful self. She looked, he realized, feeling an uncomfortable pressure in his chest, afraid.

Mme Revol glanced up, pointed her paring knife at Philippe, and said, "Make sure *you* don't get distracted."

ON THE TRAIN TO ANNECY

Philippe hoped the couple remembered the instructions Madame Créneau had given them:

During the whole day and night of the train journey, and in the railway station waiting rooms, pretend to be asleep as much as you can. Don't let anybody start a conversation with you. If somebody seems to keep staring at you, pretend to fall asleep. Don't chat with your companion in your own language. You will have a chance to relax and talk to each other during the various stops you will make at the homes of friends of your guide.

If you lose sight of your guide, don't worry. He'll be back as soon as he can. If you are arrested but your guide isn't, you must leave without giving any sign that you know him.

After midnight, the train car went quite silent, most of the passengers asleep. Philippe stared past the sleeping man next to him at the rain lashing the window—the rivulets of water made silvery streaks down the outside of the glass. Beyond that there was darkness. He tried to focus on the next steps: bus to Collonges-sous-Salève, where they'd rest at the abbé's house, but his mind was still on Céleste. He thought again of watching her walk by. He recognized that way of walking—arms held close to the body, shoulders raised. Yes, he was convinced she'd been nervous. Maybe outright scared. Why?

He became aware of movement at the back of the car and heard voices. Glancing behind him, he saw two German military policemen checking identification papers. Okay, he thought, all right. It happened often on this train; he'd been through it many times before. The light was dim and it was hard to see anything very clearly. That helped. But it was always a delicate moment.

He glanced three rows ahead of him where Armand and Lucile pretended to be asleep. He was sure they were not.

"*Carte d'identité?*" the policeman demanded in German-accented French, holding out his hand toward Philippe. Philippe reached into his pocket and pulled out the card—false, of course. He'd done this a good twenty times before and had never been challenged, and assumed he wouldn't be this time. He wasn't. The policeman handed him back his card, then checked his seatmate's.

Then the policeman worked his way down the aisle until at last he approached Armand and Lucile.

Now was the dangerous moment. If the police tried to speak to the couple. If they questioned their papers. So many things could go wrong.

Straining to hear, Philippe tried to still his breathing and make his heart stop thumping in his ears for a moment, while also trying to appear nonchalant.

The hardest part of having your guard up was making it

look like you didn't, Philippe thought as he watched the policeman scrutinize the couple's papers. The man squinted at the documents for a good while before handing them back. Philippe was just about to exhale when Lucile cleared her throat as if to speak. The policeman turned back toward her and, without meaning to, Philippe sat bolt-upright, thinking, and possibly mouthing the words, *Don't speak!*

Lucile waved her hand at the policeman as if to say, *Nothing! Nothing!* And he turned away and continued down the aisle.

Philippe slumped back and waited for his breathing to settle. He noticed his seatmate staring at him with a look of irritation. Philippe gave him a weak smile, and the man settled back in his seat, closed his eyes, and promptly fell asleep. Now that the check was complete, Philippe thought that maybe even *he* could sleep. But he found himself once again caught up in thoughts of Céleste. He realized it wasn't *all* professional concern. He guessed he really liked her. *She's out of your reach,* he told himself. *She's from Paris. Those fashionable clothes she wears. Real shoes. Her family has money. And yours does not.* He resolved to think only one last thought about her before falling asleep. The thought was this: *Whatever you're up to, Céleste, please be careful.*

CÉLESTE'S JOURNEY

A tiny slip of tissue paper. A tiny slip of paper so dangerous that if military police made a check on the train, she was to swallow it. Léon had said so.

Céleste sat on the edge of her seat on the train, jiggling her knees or trying not to jiggle them, gnawing her fingernails or trying not to gnaw them. She imagined a pulsing glow emitting from her left foot where the message was tucked into her stocking.

She had concentrated so exclusively on this little scrap of paper that when she'd seen Philippe in the station at Dunières, it had taken a few moments to register who he was. By that time she was past him, without a greeting or anything.

That was likely for the best: He was wearing his Scout uniform, and that probably meant he was on some kind of mission. She wasn't supposed to know that, but she did. And she was on a mission, too. Better not to notice each other, she'd told herself. So she'd squared her shoulders and marched on, headed to the train.

Now she jiggled and gnawed and tried not to, until the train unexpectedly came to a halt. An alert sounded, and the cry went out: "Bombers overhead!"

"*Allez-y!* Get going!" people shouted as they hurried to evacuate. They practically climbed over one another in their scramble to get off the train.

Céleste joined the crush of passengers stumbling over the tracks, her consciousness still focused on the imagined pressure of the paper against her left ankle. The roar of the approaching airplanes' engines sent everyone into the brush that lined the tracks.

Crouched with the others, Céleste squeezed her eyes shut as the planes roared overhead. The bombs whistled down and exploded in a series of deafening blasts, each blast shaking the ground under them and producing clouds of dust, smoke, and debris. Instead of covering her ears as she should have, she clutched her ankles, as if to protect that little piece of paper.

After just a few frightening moments, the planes roared away, and a strange quiet resumed—a fuzzy emptiness in her head.

"Next time, cover your ears," someone shouted at her, though his voice sounded distant and murky. "Don't worry," he added, still shouting, "your hearing will come back."

For the next few days, as she made her patchwork way across the countryside to meet her contact, there was a hissing *shhh* in her ears, and the voices of those around her on the trains and buses she rode seemed far away. At least that made it easier to ignore the conversations and the crying babies and squabbling children all around her. And trying to sleep while standing in the train corridor or sitting on her suitcase—every train and bus was so crowded!

She could think of nothing but the knot in her stomach, and that little piece of paper she had taken from her stocking and moved to her pocket. The urge to fiddle with it was almost overpowering, but she didn't want to draw attention, so she sat, telling herself over and over, "Don't touch it. Don't think about it," alternating with repeating the message to herself: *Jean will be at the Pierrou party, and he will bring three gifts.* She'd had to memorize the message in case she was forced to swallow the paper. All she knew was that it pertained to a parachute drop, where it would be, and what it would bring. And even though it was in code, there was always the danger the Germans could decipher it, putting lives in jeopardy.

Then it happened. Down the corridor came two men in leather jackets and felt hats. Gestapo! she thought, slipping the message from her pocket, pretending to cough, and popping the paper into her mouth. Chewing, chewing, chewing. Then swallowing, swallowing, swallowing.

The two men passed by without even glancing at her. And now she had tissue paper stuck between her teeth.

Finally, taking a roundabout series of trains and buses, none of them direct, since bombs had taken out stations and tracks, tunnels and bridges, she reached the village where she'd been told to contact a Monsieur Mouroux, who was to take her the rest of the way. She found a telephone booth with a working telephone, inserted the required centimes, and dialed his number.

"That's forty kilometers from here!" he protested when she told him where she wanted to go. "And all I have for transportation is a tandem bike."

"I'm sorry," she said, "but—"

"And," he cut her off, "I went there just the day before yesterday!"

She paused, not knowing what to say. She'd been on trains or buses or waiting in stations or hiding in bushes for four days. She figured she could hang on the phone a little longer.

After a long silence, the man said, "Fine. Come to my house tonight. Eleven o'clock."

Monsieur Mouroux was standing outside, holding the handlebars of his bike, when Céleste arrived. He strapped her mostly empty suitcase onto the bumper, not even raising an eyebrow at the weightlessness of it. Then she got onto the back seat, Mouroux got onto the front, and they set off into the night.

Through the sleeping village they went, the ticking of their tires echoing against the walls of the stone houses. Soon the road passed between a row of plane trees, and for a few moments, the bicycle coasted among the shadows, then shot out into moonlit countryside. Past the shuttered windows of sleeping farmhouses, past the dark lumps of cows lying in fields, past horses quietly swishing their tails.

It was lovely to be awake and alive in the night, moving through the lavender-and-thyme-scented air, listening to the whir of the wheels, the wind in her ears, inhaling the smell of the countryside, of green growing things. Of kitchen gardens growing the herbs to season future stews.

Wrapped in the blue silk of moonlight, she felt . . . She

couldn't explain how she felt. Whatever it was, she drank it in, breathed it in, felt it rush across her skin. What *was* she feeling?

Words from one of her pastor's sermons came back to her. It was something she'd thought of often since that day, the day after France surrendered to Germany on June 22, 1940.

It had been a Sunday, and outside the church, people wandered about like hens, with a certain aimlessness of purpose—as if they didn't know what to do or where to go. Go inside? Or stay outside, blinking in the June sun? And clucking like hens:

"France capitulated, surrendered."

"De Gaulle is gone—to England."

"Germany occupying the northern part of France."

"And what will happen here? Surely the government here will have to collaborate with the Nazis."

This is what people were saying, but what everyone was feeling was: What will become of us? Will we be engulfed in war? Will the tanks and bombs and machine guns find their way even here? Are we to be ruled by a totalitarian regime? By fascists? And who will we be in the face of this horror?

Céleste was nearly vaporous with fear. Her mind, like everyone else's, was whirling with anxiety and questions. Her hands were cold, though it was a warm day, and she tucked them under her armpits, which made her mother give her a little disapproving shake of the head.

How her legs carried her into the church she couldn't say. Somehow, she found herself inside, the familiarity of the cool granite slabs underfoot helping to tamp down the anxiety. The sound of the organ filled the big open space all the way to the vaulted ceiling, as if to leave not a crack for doubt or fear.

Both pastors were there, in full pastoral dress, indicating their solidarity in whatever was going to be said. When Pastor Autin climbed the stairs to the pulpit, the congregation fell silent. And when he began to speak, you could have heard a pin drop.

"We must be on our guard against believing and spreading the word that all is lost," he said. "It is not true that all is lost. Gospel truth is not lost. The word of God is not lost. Faith is not lost."

Céleste pressed her eyes shut. "All is not lost," she repeated.

"The duty of Christians," Pastor Autin said, "is to resist the violence directed at our consciences with the weapons of the spirit. We must do our duty without conceding defeat, without servility, without cowardice. We will resist when our enemies demand that we act in ways that go against the teachings of the Gospel. We will resist without fear, without pride, and without hatred."

"We will resist," Céleste whispered to herself. "Without fear."

After that sermon, Céleste had felt calm. Here was someone who knew what to do. Even if the whole world had gone mad, there was one man who knew what was right and was determined to live it. She felt a sense of purpose. She felt that everyone felt the same way, although no one spoke of it again. They simply began to live it.

Now, as she and M. Mouroux pedaled deeper into the night, the anxiety she'd felt for days peeled off her shoulders and drifted away like a loose scarf, disappearing into the darkness. Her constant companion, fear, which had clung to her with its sticky fingers, was at last torn away in a rush of acceleration as the bike sped downhill and over a bridge. The last shreds float-ed away as they coasted through wide fields with mountains rising beyond, hazy and distant. Gone.

Wasn't it ironic, she thought, that it had taken doing the thing she feared the most to lose her fear?

The road leveled; they resumed pedaling. At least a couple of hours must have passed by the time Monsieur Mouroux turned onto a smaller, rocky road and a little later onto an even smaller, rockier trail. They were still bumping along as best they could when a figure stepped out of the trees ahead of them and shouted, "*Halte!*"

THE BARN

Céleste's heart came to a shuddering stop along with the bicycle. Mouroux put a foot on the ground to steady the bike. Céleste's foot touched ground awkwardly a moment later.

"Come with me," the man said, his voice as rough as his appearance. Céleste couldn't help but notice the rifle slung over his shoulder.

Céleste and Mouroux followed him into a farmyard, and from there into the barn, wheeling the bicycle with them. Her suitcase, empty except for a change of clothes, she left strapped to the back.

Lacking moonlight, it was darker inside, but it didn't take Céleste long to realize that the barn was not full of animals. The smell of damp wool, unwashed bodies, dirty hair, and the breath of many people who'd consumed a great deal of garlic and a certain amount of wine hung in the air. Instead of the snoring of animals, she heard a soft cough, then the sounds of people rising from sleep. There was the flare of a match, the glow of a lantern being lit, and soon the red pinpricks of lit cigarettes surrounded her.

Faces emerged from the gloom—men's faces. Rough, unshaven men, all talking at once.

"Are you hungry?"

"We could make you a sandwich."

"Thirsty?"

"The boss will be back in the morning. You can talk to him then."

"Shh, leave her alone so she can go to sleep!"

Céleste let out her breath—which felt as if she'd been holding it for days. These were friends! The men and boys who'd joined the resistance. They were *maquisards*, tough as the thickets, woods, and mountain terrain for which they were named. They could also be, apparently, thoughtful and kind, Céleste noted, as they came carrying food, water, and piles of blankets. Even a pillow!

Now she felt her exhaustion. The thought of stretching out with a blanket and a pillow after days of cramped travel and hours of bicycling was so heavenly she almost swooned.

She noticed M. Mouroux lugging away a blanket of his own, chuckling a little as he went to find a spot to sleep for himself.

The *maquisards* went off to their sleeping places, several of them without their bedcovers now, she supposed, and the barn grew still.

Covered in warm blankets, with the fragrance of the night still in her hair, Céleste thought once more of the feeling that had come over her on the bike ride. That feeling—what was it? Hope, she thought, before drifting into sleep. It must be hope.

AT THE BORDER

Philippe rolled off the couch at the abbé's house, tucked in his shirt, and splashed water on his face to wake up. Then he checked to make sure his travelers were ready. They were, fully dressed and nervously waiting for the priest to return from his reconnaissance to tell them the coast was clear.

Philippe and his travelers had arrived earlier in the day and, from the attic window of the abbé's home, had looked out at green, rolling hills dotted with cows and, farther away, a few chalets. One could not fail to notice the barbed-wire fence separating them from the peaceful idyll. From the look on the couple's faces, Philippe knew he did not need to tell them that between this house and those green hills there was still plenty of danger: patrols to dodge, border guards to avoid, and that endless stretch of barbed wire to negotiate.

He reminded them again what they had been told when they'd left Les Lauzes: *You'll have to leave behind your suitcase and belongings. I can't take you and your bags. You have to go under the barbed wire one at a time, and you mustn't worry about your companion. Once you are in Switzerland, don't talk about how you got there, your guide, or the people who helped you.*

"The border of France and Switzerland is patrolled by French and Swiss, of course," Philippe said, "but you can't rule out running into German military police."

The door opened and the abbé came in, breathless from hurrying to tell them the patrol had passed. "The next one will be in about twenty minutes," he said. "Go now!"

Philippe turned to the couple, noting the pallor of their faces. "It will go fine," he said, encouraging them, "as long as we all keep our heads. Now follow me—at a distance, as usual."

He stepped outside first and walked down the dirt driveway and onto the gravel road, listening to the crunch of his footfalls and little else.

It took all his willpower not to look back to see if Armand and Lucile were following. Since he could neither hear nor see them, they must have been trailing well behind. That was fine, as long as they caught up to him before the patrol did.

When he arrived at the bigger, asphalt road, he stopped and waited, relieved to see the road was empty and the patrol nowhere in sight. And even more relieved when he heard the couple coming up behind him.

"Lie down in the ditch, there," he whispered, pointing to the ditch on one side of the road. "Stay completely still until the next patrol passes by—probably in about five minutes. Don't get up until I come and get you."

The couple disappeared down into the ditch. Philippe

settled himself on his belly in the ditch on the other side of the road.

This was the time he reviewed what would happen once the patrol passed by, but, unbidden, the picture of Céleste walking with her suitcase crossed his mind for the umpteenth time. He really hoped she wasn't doing anything illegal. She was too young to be taking such risks, he thought, then imagined her laughing at him for thinking that. "I'm as old as you!" she'd say, and he'd say, "No you're not." Then she'd say, "Nearly!" and let loose with her silvery laugh. At sixteen she was a year younger than Philippe. That seemed ages younger somehow. Plus, she was a girl. Ooh, it would really get her dander up if he were to say *that* to her!

He became aware that the dew had seeped through his clothes, giving him a chill. How much time had passed? What was going on? He'd lost track of time and now wondered . . . was it taking too long?

It was quiet. Too quiet. It would be better if there was a little wind to rustle the leaves—some noise to help cover any sound they might make. Then, as he was thinking this, there came the thudding of boots on pavement, each footfall like the ticking of a time bomb. *Tick. Tick. Tick. Thud. Thud. Thud.* The sound grew closer. Philippe smelled cigarette smoke, heard low voices murmuring—he couldn't make out the words.

At last the footsteps and voices receded. Philippe got up and signaled to his travelers in the ditch to follow him.

Across the asphalt.

"Shh!" Philippe whispered.

To the fence.

"Be careful," Philippe instructed as he held the wire for Armand. "As soon as you're under," he instructed, "run. Don't wait for Lucile. Run to the first Swiss soldier you see. Make sure he's Swiss."

Armand was through, and running, disappearing into the darkness. Good.

Next Lucile. Philippe lifted the wire and she started to crawl under it. Philippe's mind flitted to Céleste's suitcase. He pictured it: her knuckles white where she gripped the handle. That suitcase wasn't full of clothes—he was sure of it. It was full of contraband. Or money.

He looked at the nurse. *Hurry up!* he thought. How long had she been struggling to get through? Once again, he'd lost track of time for a moment.

The crack of a rifle shot nearly lifted him off his feet. Then shouts: *"Arrêtez"* (French) and *"Achtung!"* (German).

Floodlights lit up the scene: the nurse's rear end, still on the French side of the border, and Philippe's face, squinting against the bright light and confused by the orders being shouted in German.

The nurse wriggled her way back to the French side of the fence—wisely. The first shot had only been a warning. But they might have shot her if she'd tried to keep going.

One of the French patrols was speaking to them. Philippe didn't have to even listen to know that he was saying, "You are under arrest."

TOO MUCH TIME TO THINK

Philippe could sleep on trains, in barns, on floors, on the damp ground. He could go for long stretches without food. He didn't mind deprivation. In fact, he kind of thrived on it.

So the hard cot in the damp jail cell, the scratchy blanket, the dull food—none of that bothered him. What bothered him most was there was too much time to think. Especially about what he didn't want to think about: His mistakes. His failures. He replayed over and over how things had gone wrong. He had gotten distracted and hadn't been paying attention. He was inept. It was his inattentiveness and impulsiveness that had gotten him into trouble. Just like his father always said it would.

He thought of his home in Normandy, the sound of the surf in his ears, and the wind whistling around the cliffs, sending spray flying from the crests of the big waves.

Before Philippe had left home, he and his father had argued. Philippe had been recording the movements of the German navy and sending information to the Allies. When his father found out, he said Philippe was like "a toddler playing with a powder keg." Philippe said that at sixteen he was old enough to know what he was doing. His father said that Philippe was putting not just himself but his whole family at risk. "Or are you too stupid to even know that?" he'd shouted.

Philippe said something back—now he couldn't remember what—that had caused his father to slap him across the face. Philippe barely felt the sting—the white-hot shock of it, the prickling ache that followed. This time his own anger had reached the boiling point. Steamlike rage whistled through him, and he put the full force of it behind his closed fist as he slammed it into his father's gut.

It felt like he'd hit a brick wall—his father still had a naval officer's physique. Philippe wondered if he'd broken his hand. Then, seeing the bigger man doubled over, he felt a momentary sense of glee—he'd actually gotten strong enough to inflict pain! Next, a sense of remorse swept over him as he realized he was now no better than his abusive father. Then fear. He'd never hit his dad before, and once the man recovered, he'd beat the stuffing out of Philippe—or kill him.

Philippe turned and ran, stopping at home only long enough to throw a few things into a bag. From there, he just kept running. And running.

Running right into jail—just like his father said he would. Because he'd been stupid. Just like his father said he was. So, in attempting to prove his father wrong, he'd proven him right. And now he had plenty of time to replay both scenes, over and over—the one with his father and the one that had just happened at the border. What he could have done differently.

What he could have said differently. He'd messed up getting the nurse over the border, probably because he got distracted.

At least she was still all right. Still in jail, but she hadn't been deported or—at least when he'd last caught a glimpse of her— beaten up. And he'd been able to warn her to keep quiet. There were often spies planted in the cells.

His thoughts were interrupted by the entrance of a couple of unfriendly-looking men. They wanted to ask him "a few questions," they said.

As they escorted him into a small bare room with unpleasantly stained walls, Philippe tried to remember something one of the Jewish boys at Sunnyside had told him.

"Relax your muscles," his friend had said, explaining how he'd withstood being beaten for seventeen hours straight. "If you tense up, you get hurt. If you can completely let your muscles relax, it doesn't hurt as much."

Philippe reminded himself of this as the two interrogators shut the door behind him.

8.
LATE JUNE 1943

PERDANT NABS JULES

Inspector Perdant sat and drummed his fingers on the steering wheel, waiting. La Crapule had not showed up for any of his preassigned meetings with Perdant, and Perdant was not about to let it go.

He knew the little rascal delivered goat cheese and things he foraged in the forest—mushrooms, berries, and the tender, curled tops of young fiddlehead ferns—to the hotel restaurant, so Perdant parked his car across the street and waited. And, there! The scoundrel was just coming out of the back door of the hotel.

Perdant stuck his head out of the car window and yelled, "La Crapule! Come with me!"

"What, *now*?" Jules said.

"Oh, I'm sorry." Perdant's voice dripped with sarcasm. "Do you have an appointment for some illegal activity? Black marketeering, perhaps?"

Jules didn't respond, and Perdant reached over and swung

the passenger-side door open. Jules got in, clutching his empty gunnysack as if he wished he could climb into it and throw himself off the nearest bridge.

"You haven't come to your meetings with me," the policeman said.

"Oh, did you mean to start *right away*?" Jules said with wide-eyed innocence.

"No, I meant next year," Perdant said. "Of course I meant to start right away! Now, what have you got for me?"

"What have I got?" Jules stared at his gunnysack.

"Information."

"What kind of information?"

"Noticed any odd behavior?" Perdant said. "Seen anything strange?"

Jules thought. "Monsieur Devidal has a cow with only one eye. And I saw some kittens just born that are all black on one side and white on the other—it's the strangest thing you ever saw."

Perdant groaned. "I'm talking about people—people!— involved in illegal activity. I know you know who they are. For instance, you know Jean-Paul Filon, right?"

"I guess maybe I met him," Jules said.

"And you know where he lives, don't you?"

Jules screwed up his face as if thinking.

"The Mousset farm, isn't it?" Perdant prodded.

Jules shrugged. "Maybe," he said.

"I know you know where it is, so let's go."

JEAN-PAUL'S PERSONAL MISSION

Jean-Paul had gotten up early that morning, not very well rested. He'd caught a cold that had migrated to his chest, and he'd awakened coughing several times in the night.

Even so, he was happier than he'd been in a long time. The anticipation of what he was going to do that day energized him, and he even sang a little song while he made his bed.

He cast his eye over the table in his room, empty except for the falsified documents he'd finished the night before. On the seat of the chair sat his rucksack, ready for the day. His jacket hung on the back of the chair.

One of the newly forged identification cards he put in his own pocket; the other documents he slid into concealed pockets inside his sleeves and the shoulders of his jacket. A demand to empty his pockets would turn up nothing. A more thorough search would be another matter, of course. For the short trip to Mme Créneau's, he could probably just carry the papers in his rucksack with his books and notebook, but better safe than sorry, he thought, as he stepped out into the cool morning air.

He glanced at his watch. A sneeze caught him in mid-glance, and he checked his pocket for his handkerchief.

He wheeled his bicycle out of the farmyard, giving a wave to M. Mousset, who was just heading into the barn. Once on the road, he got the bike rolling and swung himself onto the seat, then coasted down the hill in the bracing air. He took a deep breath in and immediately started coughing. He coughed so hard he had to pull over and stop until the coughing fit passed. What if he started coughing like that in class? He didn't want to go all the way to Clermont-Ferrand and spend the class period in the hall, coughing. Nor did he want to disrupt class or in any way draw attention to himself. He simply wanted—badly, powerfully, achingly, overwhelmingly—to become a doctor. And now, thanks to his forgery skills, he had transformed himself into Jean-Paul Lafour, medical student.

He'd have to stop at the pharmacy and get some throat lozenges. As long as everything went smoothly, he'd still have time to drop off the papers before he had to catch the train.

Everything did not go smoothly. There was already a line at the pharmacy. The elderly lady ahead of him went on and on about how she used to get the little white pills, but now the pharmacist gave her the big brown pills, which were hard to swallow, and what happened to the little white pills she used to have?

Jean-Paul shifted from one foot to the other, impatiently rattling a small tin box of lozenges.

Finally, after he'd paid for the lozenges, he got back onto his bike and headed for the drop-off spot. Almost immediately, the bike chain fell off, and he had to stop and fix it. Then he wiped the grease off his hands with a rag he kept for the purpose and checked his watch.

The shrill whistle of the train announced that it was nearing the station.

He stood for a moment, weighing the pros and cons. If he was going to catch the train, he did not have time to drop the papers. That was too bad, since it would be a couple of days before he had a break from classes and could get back—it was a long train ride to Clermont-Ferrand, and he'd arranged to stay with a contact there. It would probably be fine to deliver them later. It wasn't ideal; he didn't much like the idea of traveling with falsified papers in his jacket sleeves all the way to a city known to be seething with Germans. But now that he'd finally managed to fake his way into medical school, he wasn't going to miss class—he had waited too long already.

He wheeled his bike up the hill to the station and bought himself a ticket just as the train chugged into sight.

PERDANT GOES HUNTING

"The thing is," Perdant said to Jules as he pulled the car over at the Mousset farm, "I should have paid more attention to what was on the sleds than what was going on inside that house."

Perdant had gone over in his mind all the people he'd met and the places he'd been these last six months. He'd gone all the way back to that first night in Les Lauzes when the kids came sledding down the hill and almost knocked him over. He probably should have arrested them all right then and there.

That was the same night he gave that young man a ticket for riding his bicycle without a light, the one who had kicked up his heels afterward. Perdant had puzzled over that ever since. But now he thought he understood. Jean-Paul Filon, also one of the sled-pulling youths who'd sung verse after verse of "The Marseillaise," was a highly suspicious character and not to be trusted.

"I've thought about it and thought about it and now I think I know," Perdant mused.

"Know what?" Jules, unaware of the workings of Perdant's memory, had no idea what he was talking about.

"What was on those sleds."

"What sleds?" Jules said, as he and Perdant walked toward the farm.

"The sleds those three kids were pulling that night. And I think I know where they were going."

"Sledding?"

"No." Perdant got out of the car and waited for Jules. "They were not going sledding. They had something on those sleds. What was it, and where did it end up?"

"Maybe it was furniture," Jules said, as he and Perdant walked toward the farm.

"No," Perdant said.

"Or school supplies," Jules offered.

"Maybe," Perdant murmured, "or maybe not."

»«

Monsieur Mousset was sitting on the edge of the stone trough in the yard, mopping his brow and tossing pine cones for a puppy to chase.

Perdant and Jules stepped into the yard, and *Bonjour*s were exchanged.

"Is there a Jean-Paul Filon living here?" Perdant asked.

"*Oui*," the farmer said.

"Is he here?"

"*Non*," was the answer.

"Do you know where he is?"

"*Non.*"

"Any idea when he will return?"

"*Non.*"

These people are maddening, Perdant thought. It was as if they feared their voices would wear out if they said more than one syllable at a time.

"Can I take a look at his room?"

The farmer casually lifted a hand to indicate the door to the boy's room, across the yard.

Jules said something to the farmer in the local patois. The farmer answered, also in patois.

Perdant turned back to them. "Use French, please," he said. "I want to know what is being said in my presence."

"The boy asked the puppy's name," the farmer explained.

"And?" Perdant asked.

"It's *Filou*," Jules said. "Trickster."

"You," he said, taking Jules by the arm and striding toward the room the farmer had indicated, "come with me."

Perdant stepped into Jean-Paul Filon's room and looked around. It was a simple room: A bed, neatly made. An extra shirt and pair of trousers. A writing desk.

"What does he use the desk for?" Perdant called over his shoulder to the farmer.

The farmer shrugged.

Perdant tapped the desk, imagining a row of colored inks, stacks of stationery, blank ration cards. He could picture engraving tools, copper, rubber, linoleum. He thought he could almost make out the outline of a typewriter on the freshly dusted desktop.

"And the sewing machine?" Perdant hollered to the farmer.

"To sew feed sacks," the farmer shouted back.

There was nothing incriminating to be found. The young man's room was so tidy, so wiped clean of everything, it was almost suspicious.

Perdant prowled through the barn and the outbuildings, poking at the straw and peeking into bins and boxes. He scoured the yard and garden, even turning over stones. Finally he paused, staring at the bees buzzing around the dozen or so white beehives at the rear of the garden.

"Come over here." Perdant waved Jules over. Once Jules was standing next to him, he said, "Apparently they know what they're doing, bees." He pointed to the beehives. "They go out searching for nectar, then come back and do a little dance to tell the others where the nectar is. A kind of a code, you might say."

"Uh-huh," Jules said.

"All you have to do is stand back and watch the dance to find the honey," Perdant mused. He stood as if watching, yet he was not watching, because there was a kind of buzzing in the back of his head, as if it were full of angry bees. Once again he had not made a successful arrest or found anything incriminating. And he supposed people were laughing, as usual, about him behind his back: *Perdant is a "loser."*

He shook his head hard as if to rid it of bees and resolved to do better next time. Better and bigger.

JEAN-PAUL,
MEDICAL STUDENT

Jean-Paul loved everything about school: the old buildings, the smell of musty books, nervous sweat, pencil shavings, chalky chalkboards, even the apple cores moldering in wastebaskets. He'd been reading anatomy books and anything else like that he could get his hands on, but now he would really start learning.

As he slid into his assigned seat and set his book and notebook on the desk, he could practically hear the whir of brains at work: new ideas, thoughts, philosophies, equations, theories, all flitting from mind to mind like songbirds in the trees. He felt good, knowing he was on the right path. He was meant to be a doctor. Maybe a surgeon, his friends had suggested.

"Such a steady hand!" Sylvie had once remarked, watching Jean-Paul forge a signature. "Imagine how he'd be with a scalpel. I'd trust him to operate on me. How about you, Céleste?"

"Not in a million years," Céleste had said, returning to her book.

The memory made him chuckle, which led to the tickle in the back of his throat that preceded a coughing fit. He quickly snapped open the box of lozenges and popped one into his mouth, feeling the chloromethylate numb his throat into submission.

The professor began his lecture, and Jean-Paul set his pen to paper with a completely clear conscience. It was ironic that he had to break the law so that he could quit an illegal occupation—forgery—to pursue a legal one. Or legal for some people. Jews had been shut out of all the professions, including medicine, teaching, government jobs, journalism. Their businesses had been "aryanized," meaning confiscated, along with their radios, telephones, even bicycles. They'd been barred from restaurants, movies, concerts, swimming pools, and forbidden to leave their houses between 8:00 p.m. and 5:00 a.m. And those were the good old days. Now they were arrested, deported, and murdered.

So, even though he was posing as an Algerian Frenchman from Alsace—a far cry from who he really was, a Latvian Jew from Nice—he did not feel guilty about anything. Far from it. What are you supposed to do when the law is morally wrong?

He turned his mind back to the lecture. Perfectly aware of the high cost and scarcity of paper, he wrote in a very small hand all the way across the paper, filling all the margins. He was just turning the page to continue his notes on the flip side when a German soldier burst into the lecture hall brandishing a submachine gun.

"*Raus! Raus!*—Out! Out!" he shouted, his voice high and raspy, sounding almost frightened himself.

There were more shouts and scuffling outside—even shots fired—as the same scene played out in classrooms up and down the corridors. In Jean-Paul's room, the students hurriedly rose and snatched up their books and papers.

In the midst of all the noise of chairs scraping the floor, shuffling feet, and books closing, Jean-Paul glimpsed a couple of students tearing up papers. His thoughts went immediately to the documents in his jacket sleeves. It would draw far too much attention to try to retrieve them, and he spent no time chastising himself over it. There was nothing he could do about it now. He had to think of how to get away without being stopped, and definitely without being searched!

The students moved out of the lecture hall, streaming toward the big staircase that led to the main floor. From the third-floor window, Jean-Paul looked down at the courtyard below swirling with hundreds of students and lecturers.

His mind pedaled through options as he shuffled along with the crowd. Jump out a window? Too high. Try to disappear in the crowd of students? Unlikely to do any good. There would be a checkpoint through which students would be funneled.

He recalled that, on the way to class, he had passed a small side stairway that probably led to a lesser-used door—at least he felt sure it didn't lead to the main entrance. To get to it, he'd have to go against the tide of students moving toward the main stairway. So he turned around and began weaving his way through the crowd, catching snatches of conversation.

"German military police . . ."

". . . looking for resisters . . ."

". . . searching for weapons and ammunition . . ."

I don't have any weapons or ammunition, he thought as he

edged sideways through the crowd, but it hardly matters—the false documents I'm carrying are enough to arrest and probably execute me. If they were to find out I'm Jewish . . . Well, he didn't want to think about it.

Jean-Paul quietly slipped around the corner and down the stairs, taking them two at a time. Before he reached the first floor, he heard voices, one of them telling a joke—in German.

"How do you confuse a Frenchman?"

"I don't know. How?"

"Give him a rifle and tell him to use it."

Laughter.

Hoping to slip away unnoticed, Jean-Paul took one backward step up the stairs.

"You, there!" a German-accented voice shouted. The shoulders and head of a uniformed soldier appeared in the stairwell below. "Come down here at once."

>> <<

Sooner than he would have liked, Jean-Paul was standing in front of the three smirking soldiers.

"Your identification card, please," said the one who either was in charge or who acted like he was.

Jean-Paul handed over his card and reminded himself to look the soldier in the eye. Stay calm. Don't do anything aggressive.

"You are a student?" the soldier asked in bad French.

"*Oui*," Jean-Paul answered, pointing to the stamp on his ID that stated MEDICAL STUDENT. He hoped the ink was thoroughly dry by now.

Starting at Jean-Paul's ankles, the soldier patted his pant

legs slowly, methodically, moving up, paying special attention to the pockets. The man lifted Jean-Paul's arms straight out in order to pat his jacket. The contents of the pocket made a distinctive rattle—exactly the sound that pistol cartridges made in their metal box.

The soldier plunged his hand into Jean-Paul's pocket, pulled out the box, and without looking at it, triumphantly held it up for his comrades to see.

They hooted with laughter. Only then did the soldier look at the box to see what he held in his hand: a tin of throat lozenges.

His friends guffawed so hard they gasped. The embarrassed soldier handed Jean-Paul his lozenges, gave him a kick in the pants, and sent him on his way.

PHILIPPE IN THE CAPTAIN'S OFFICE

The door to the police captain's office opened, and sunlight swept over Philippe like a searchlight picking out a prison escapee.

The captain sat behind a big desk, slicing through envelopes with a brass letter opener that glinted from the light streaming through the window.

"Shut the door when you go out," the police captain said to the gendarme who had ushered Philippe into the room.

The gendarme retreated, pulling the door shut behind him.

Philippe stood alone in front of the big desk, feeling as if he were waiting to have punishment doled out by his father. He touched a bruise on his face and ran his tongue over his teeth, then clenched those teeth to prevent years of pent-up rage from spilling out of his mouth.

He thought about the moment when he had hit his father.

Lashing out like that, with fists, the way his father did—that was the coward's way. He wanted to be better than that. Bigger than that. Stronger than that.

So now he looked at the top of the captain's head as the man sliced open another letter. Philippe wondered if he could relax his mind the way he had relaxed his muscles. He imagined himself standing in the ocean, letting the surf roll over him, feeling the cool water quell the fire that raged inside.

Without looking up, the captain said, "I don't know what you've done that's brought you in front of me." He looked up, his gaze at first hard, but softening as he looked at Philippe. He stared at the boy for a long moment, then said with a slight smile, "But I congratulate you."

Congratulate me? Philippe thought. Had he heard that right? Was the captain being sarcastic?

"I'm going to release you," the man said gently, "but I'm telling you . . ." He paused to aim the pointed end of the opener at Philippe. "I don't ever want to see you again."

Philippe was so unprepared for this response that he simply stood in front of the desk, unsure of what to do next.

"*And.*" The policeman stared intently at Philippe as he emphasized each word of the next sentence. "You must stop doing this kind of work." Barely pausing, he said, "You are free to go," and he waved Philippe away before slashing at another piece of mail. Philippe walked out in a daze.

He stayed in the area only long enough to see that Lucile was also released and to make a contact for her—someone else would see her to Switzerland.

Then he headed straight for the train station, planning to

sleep the entire day it would take to get to Les Lauzes, and wondering . . . Would Céleste be there?

Céleste was walking along the platform at the last train station before Les Lauzes when she felt some small sharp thing biting into the sole of her foot. She set her suitcase on an empty flatbed car attached to an idle train, then slipped off her shoe and found what had been irritating her: a little stone. As she was shaking it out, the train to which the flatcar was attached started moving—with her suitcase still on it.

The suitcase that was no longer empty. The *maquisards* had filled it with . . . Well, she didn't know, because she hadn't dared to look inside since. But if that suitcase were to be intercepted and opened by the wrong people . . .

One shoe on and one shoe off, her heart in her throat and her mind in disarray, she dashed away, chasing after the train.

9.
JUNE 30, 1943
LES LAUZES

THE YELLOW SUITCASE

Céleste couldn't have said what had awakened her and drawn her to the window. There was little to see—only the faintest milky light leaking along the edge of the horizon and the morning stars trembling in the still-dark sky. She could just make out the familiar outline of Les Lauzes: the forested hill rising sharply from the river, and above that, stone walls and buildings, the steepled church. Everything looked right.

But there was something . . . something not right. She unlatched the windows and opened them out. Disturbed by the sound, a couple of mourning doves scuttled on the roof above.

Something had awakened her. Maybe it was the suitcase she currently had stashed under her bed that she couldn't stop thinking about. The yellow suitcase that she'd brought from Paris three years earlier, filled with summer frocks for her vacation, was now filled with, well, Céleste didn't know, but for sure it wasn't dresses!

It had been empty when she'd left Les Lauzes on her mission, but on her way back the suitcase was full—and heavy. On all the train rides it had taken to get back to Les Lauzes, she'd never been so nervous in her entire life. Then it had almost been carried away by that flatbed car. She'd had to run to catch up to it.

The remainder of the trip, she sat on the suitcase, steadfastly refusing to take off her shoe to shake out yet another stone that had somehow wiggled its way inside. She resolved that, when she got home, she'd sleep for sixteen hours and do nothing dangerous ever again.

Yet here she was, a scant six hours later, dreamily staring out the window in the predawn stillness. The other girls on her floor were still asleep—their hair spread out prettily on their pillows, open mouths breathing softly.

And then it came to her—what was wrong. A sound. The hum of motors. Car engines. Now distinct as they emerged from around the hill: One, two, three dark sedans whizzed by so fast that once they were gone, Céleste doubted she had seen them. Next a canvas-sided truck lumbered past, then disappeared. She might have thought she'd imagined it all except for the reason her heart was still racing . . . swastikas.

"Get up! Get up!" she hollered, pulling a sweater over her pajamas. "Raid!"

There was no way of knowing where the cars were headed—to what residence, what farm, what house?

Covers were thrown back, clothes pulled on, feet slipped into shoes. Bodies pounded down the stairs, slipped out the back door, and ran along the narrow walkways and paths that led to the forested hill beyond the village.

Once Henni and the others were out of the house, Céleste sat down on her bed. Trying to get rid of the swirly feeling in her head, she leaned over and put her head between her legs. There, under the bed, was the suitcase she was supposed to deliver to the château where she'd met Léon. What was she going to do about *that*?

RAID ON RIVER HOUSE

Perdant had planned to bide his time concentrating on "maintaining positive relationships with the locals" while he waited for word from police headquarters about carrying out his proposed raid. So he was taken by surprise when he was informed that a raid was in process at River House, on Chemin du Dragon. Already. Without him.

By the time Perdant arrived, even from outside the house he could hear thumps and thuds and shouts of *"Schwein Jude—* Jewish pig!" He winced, then entered.

The place was crowded with plainclothes German military police—or whoever they were—every one of them with a weapon in hand. The number of machine guns caused even Perdant's heart to race.

The thug shouting *"Schwein Jude"* was openly beating a young man. Perdant looked away.

Who were they? Gestapo? Kripo—criminal police? Or German military police? Who had directed the raid? Head of Gestapo in Lyon, Klaus Barbie? Wehrmacht?

"Who sent you?" Perdant asked, trying to keep his voice level. The presence of so many machine guns and the casual brutality—a boy was being shoved, by the barrel of a gun, into another room as he asked this question—made him quake a little.

The more senior member turned his reptilian head to regard Perdant with his cold gray eyes. "And who are you?" he asked.

Perdant told him and handed him his card.

"Ah, yes, the boy policeman." The German sniffed at his card and set it on a side table. "We have been informed that this house is harboring wanted terrorists." He rattled a piece of paper at Perdant. "We come and what do we find? A nest of Jews and anti-patriots! And, of course, these . . . these . . ." The man gestured at the gathered boys while searching for the French word.

"*Les étudiants?*" Perdant suggested. "Students?"

The man scoffed. "Terrorists," he spat out.

Perdant couldn't prevent a slight lift of his eyebrows, and the man responded with a disdainful curl of his lip. "Since you haven't investigated it yourself," the German said, "then we must do it, to keep your little village safe. For the safety of all."

The student boarders were taken, one by one, into a separate room to be interrogated while the rest were held in the dining room, waiting their turn. Perdant did a quick head count and was pretty sure that some of the students were missing—perhaps they had fled to the woods. He decided not to mention it.

From the living room—now the interrogation room—came

a snarling voice and muffled noises Perdant didn't want to think about. The student emerged with a bloodied face that made Perdant turn away. There was nothing he could do here, nothing he could say, no one he could help. The Germans didn't want help from him, nor did he want to give it.

So he went out, walking the wooded path along the river, hoping he would not see anyone he didn't want to see.

Perdant found he was trembling. Was it because his authority had been usurped? That he hadn't been consulted? That he, himself, hadn't been the one to make these arrests?

Maybe. Or maybe it was the brutality of the raid. And the fact that he had finally accepted where these kids would be sent: not to a new homeland in Poland where they could live in peace. That is what everyone had been told, and it was still an idea to which many people clung. He had believed that myth—or had chosen to believe it—for a long time, but he could no longer deny the truth: These young people would be sent to their deaths.

He followed the path to a quiet place and, as he had as a child, started throwing rock after rock into the river. He tried to derive some satisfaction from the ache in his arm, from the *thunk* as the rock hit the water, and the way the stone disappeared from view, knowing it was sinking down, down, down, and he would never see it again. Each stone a bad decision he had made.

The decision to join the national police.

His desire for promotion that had led him here.

His fawning admiration for the leaders of Vichy and, worse, their German overlords.

It seemed, if he was going to be honest about it, that he, like everyone else around here, didn't much care for the German occupiers.

Why? he wondered. Why did he want to do what he did? He'd had the idea that he would help rid France of foreign troublemakers, communists, Bolsheviks, and Jews. He'd thought he was helping to save Europe from a terrible conspiracy, and helping to restore France to its former greatness through the goals championed by Marshal Pétain and the Vichy government: "Work, Family, Fatherland."

He didn't know what to believe anymore, except that he'd seen these kids on their sleds and bikes, singing as they hiked in the woods. They were hardly dangerous. They were just kids! All they wanted was to have a life.

Still . . . Perdant brushed the grit off the palms of his hands and straightened his back. He was not going to be shown up by some German hoodlums. He was going to show his superiors he could make a few arrests, too. Not in the thuggish way the Germans did it, but in civilized French fashion. He'd been mulling a variety of things he'd heard here and there—and had begun putting it together. It added up to criminal activity that he intended to investigate. All he needed was someone to show him the way.

The scoundrel. He went to find him.

NOT INVISIBLE ENOUGH

The afternoon sun slanted in through the hotel dining room windows, laying elegant white stripes across the linen table-cloths.

Jules had been practicing being invisible, a talent he figured would come in handy for avoiding Perdant. Unfortunately, his *sabots* tick-tocking across the tile would have given him away. If there had been anyone there to notice.

But nobody was there—well, *almost* nobody. Only a lady wearing a long, swishy skirt who brushed past him, limping slightly, and who paused only long enough for him to slip a note into her hand before she disappeared out the door into a blinding shaft of sunlight.

Now the dining room was empty and quiet. Jules took advantage of its emptiness to filch a handful of sugar lumps from a china bowl before pushing through the swinging door to the kitchen.

The enticing and all-too-unfamiliar smell of melting chocolate drew him to a double boiler on the stove, the bubbling chocolate the only sound in the also empty kitchen. In fact, the whole place was as quiet as the palace in the fairy story where everybody fell asleep for one hundred years. Well, thought Jules, even if the enchantment only lasted for a few moments, it would be long enough to stick his finger into the pot and—

"Ouch!" It was as if the chocolate bit him! He jerked his burned finger out of the pot and stuck it into his mouth, singeing his tongue.

And now someone had him by the scruff of the neck and was shuttling him toward the kitchen door.

"Chanterelles!" he managed to squeak out, holding up the basket he was carrying.

The basket of mushrooms was snatched out of his hand, and he very swiftly found himself out on the street.

"What about my payment?" he squawked.

"Come back tomorrow," said the cook.

"And my basket!" Jules cried.

"Tomorrow," the cook repeated, and shut the door.

The rest of the hotel staff was outside, animatedly discussing the morning's event: a raid on one of the houses.

A raid! Jules thought. It was the first he'd heard of it. He sensed the dark mood of the hotel staff. Some were smoking nervously; others tucked their hands under their armpits and leaned against the building. He thought of the cook's unusual snappishness. Perhaps it explained the quiet of the dining room. The day, which had seemed so bright, dimmed a little. And to make matters worse, he noticed that policeman, Perdant, eyeing him from across the street.

"La Crapule!" Inspector Perdant shouted. "Come over here."

Does he know about the sugar lumps? Jules wondered. He deposited them into the safety of his pocket, then crossed the street to where Perdant waited, leaning against his car.

"What do you know about Château de Roque?" Perdant asked him.

"That place?" Jules said. "It's been empty for years."

"Yeah, well, it might not be so empty anymore. And it sounds like you know it, so get in."

Perdant opened the car door and shooed Jules into the front passenger seat. He went around to the driver's side, opened his door, and slid inside. Before starting the car, he reached over Jules to open the glove box, where he deposited his sidearm, a semiautomatic service pistol.

GESTAPO!

Word spread: It was the Gestapo.

The Gestapo! Céleste thought as she pushed her bike up one of the steeper village streets. A new level of horror. The Gestapo was merciless in its pursuit of information—they wouldn't quit until those in custody gave up names. Names and addresses.

Céleste, Sylvie, and Henni converged on Madame Créneau's at the same time. When the door opened, the aroma of cooking fruit rushed out while Madame pulled them inside.

Everyone started talking at once.

"Gestapo—River House—" Celeste began while Sylvie was saying, "—some of the boys are in the woods—" and Henni cried, "Max's friend was staying there—they took him! Max is in danger now!"

"Everyone sit down and we'll get it all sorted," Mme Créneau said while filling a teakettle with water.

Céleste noticed Madame's hand shaking as she lit the stove and set the kettle on to boil. It wasn't until she sat down at the kitchen table herself that Céleste realized her own legs were trembling. But she found herself steadied by the velvety feel of the steamy kitchen, the smell of jam cooking on the stove, and the empty jars lining the countertop waiting to be filled. It was all so normal, and seemed somehow hopeful.

"Now," Mme Créneau said, taking off her apron. "What happened?"

Sylvie told them about going to River House and seeing those who were arrested come outside; she counted the students as they came down the stairs and climbed into the truck. Eighteen. And the director of the house, too. But still, *that was not everyone*.

"Not everyone?" Mme Créneau said.

"The household had been warned," Sylvie explained. "But some of them felt more secure in the house than others. Some spent the night in the woods. Some chose not to."

The three girls all started firing questions at once:

"Is the Gestapo gone for good?"

"What if they come back?"

"Is this likely to keep happening?"

Mme Créneau held up her hand to stop them and said, "No one knows the answers to any of those questions. We just have to get as many people to safety as we can. The Gestapo is likely to get the names of others who were in the house, so we must help those young men first."

"And Max!" Henni chimed in. "His friend was arrested and knows where Max is staying."

"And you, Henni," Céleste said. "His friend knows about you, too."

"And Madeleine," Henni said.

"You and they will need somewhere to stay for a short time until we can get everything arranged. Now . . . Where to take them?" Mme Créneau drummed her index finger against her chin, thinking. Her gaze fell on Céleste. "Do you know anywhere, Céleste?"

Céleste's urge was to go home, climb into bed, and pull the covers over her head. *No*, a part of her wanted to say, *I don't know any place*. But the thought of the remote, abandoned hillside château came to her, its vine-covered turret, the old orchard grown up with grass, the Scotch broom growing in the garden, the gate hanging on its hinges. And she remembered the suitcase that was to be delivered there.

While Céleste's mind lingered on this image, Mme Créneau was thinking out loud. "Jean-Paul seems to have disappeared . . . He was supposed to deliver papers for Max . . . Has anybody seen him?"

None of them had seen Jean-Paul.

"Has anybody seen Jules?"

None of them had seen Jules.

Everything is falling apart! Céleste thought. Jean-Paul had disappeared. Jules was nowhere to be found. The Gestapo had raided one of the houses! What else could go wrong?

Mme Créneau asked Sylvie about the young men who had spent the night in the woods.

"I know where to look for them," Sylvie said, reminding

Céleste that there was something to do. And as long as there was something to do, there was still hope.

"And I know a place where they can stay," Celeste said. She told them about the château.

"I hadn't thought of that," Mme Créneau said. "These boys are old enough to be left on their own, but they'll still need someone to move them out of the country."

"Philippe?" Céleste suggested.

Madame turned her gaze on Céleste. "You haven't heard," she said softly.

"What?" Céleste's throat was so constricted she could barely manage the word.

"He was arrested."

Céleste turned her head to look out the window and blinked away tears. The day that had begun so sweetly before the arrival of the German police was still bright, but the brightness seemed metallic, as if the sunlight had a knife-sharp edge.

But now she had to pay attention, because Madame was giving her an assignment:

"Céleste," she said. "You must find Jean-Paul and ask him to make new papers for the others. While you're at it, get Max's papers, then get Max and take him to the château. That's a lot," she said. "Will you be able to handle all that?"

Céleste nodded. And the suitcase, she thought. Don't forget the suitcase.

"And in case you meet anyone who is thinking of revenge, you must spread the word," Mme Créneau said. "There must be no retaliation. Not against Germans. Not against Perdant. Nothing can be allowed to jeopardize the rescue operation."

Céleste nodded again. The ramifications of what had happened were clear. If someone were to try to retaliate for the raid or do anything that seemed like it, the Germans would hit back a hundred times harder. It had happened in other places, other villages.

Madame continued with the plan. Sylvie was to find the other boys—the ones who had slept in the woods—and meet Céleste and Max at the château.

"As for me," Mme Créneau said, "I'll take Henni and Madeleine to a safer place. But first, Henni and I have to finish this jam," she said, tying on her apron. "I used my entire sugar ration, and I'm not going to see it ruined!"

PERDANT AND JULES
LOOK FOR THE CHÂTEAU

"Why do you want to go to the château?" Jules asked Perdant. "Was it something Claude said? Because you know he's kind of . . ." Jules tapped the side of his head to indicate *crazy*.

"I don't need to divulge my sources to you, nor will I," Perdant said.

While Jules wondered what *divulge* meant, Perdant stopped the car at the intersection of the main road that led out of town.

"All I need," the policeman went on, "is for you to get me to the château. Which way?"

Jules pointed to the right, and while Perdant swung the car to the right, Jules plunged his hands into his jacket pockets and fingered the sugar lumps he had filched from the hotel dining room. He thought of the dessert he'd glimpsed as he passed through the kitchen—a delicious little mountain of Chantilly cream next to a bowl of jewel-like strawberries. He tried to imagine what it would taste like but really couldn't. Something like that was only for wealthy tourists or German officers. And as for the melted chocolate, what was to be *its* destiny?

Clutching the steering wheel, Perdant stared out the windshield and muttered, "Someone has to keep law and order, am I right?"

"I don't know," Jules said. "Somehow we got along without a policeman before you got here."

Perdant scoffed. "You got along, that's for sure. Everybody in cahoots. You can find more criminals here than ever were in the Bastille."

"Turn here," Jules said.

Perdant spun the wheel, turning the Citroën onto something that could hardly be considered a road. They bumped over rocks and roots, but Perdant seemed oblivious.

"And!" he continued, nearly shouting with frustration. "Not only are there Jewish children mixed in with the Protestants and Catholics at the homes and schools, but some of the teachers, cooks, and directors of the homes are Jewish, too. Those sweet little Protestant children in those pews on Christmas Day live with Jewish children in the children's homes. But, like every other frustratingly silent person in this place, they keep their mouths shut. Maybe I didn't know it then, but I figured it out, La Crapule, and now I'm on to all of them!"

Ahead, Jules saw a road going off to the left that, after the recent rains, was probably in pretty bad shape.

"Turn left here," he told Perdant.

"I didn't know it then, but if I had arrested everyone at that Christmas service who was involved in illegal activities, I'd have had to arrest nearly the entire congregation. That stout lady who was sitting in the pew in front of me?" Perdant said. "I've seen her lugging cauldrons of soup to the parsonage, no doubt to help feed all the criminals passing through the pastor's home. And it's not just him! I bet all twelve of the pastors on the plateau are involved. On top of that, the farmers either have, are, or soon will be hiding Jews, labor service dodgers, and miscellaneous troublemakers."

The car galumphed over a large rock.

"Why do you people do this? Is it pure belligerence?" Perdant raved on. "Do you enjoy defying the law—and common sense? Does everybody want to risk their lives? Does nobody realize how much they put themselves and their families at risk? Or are they too stupid to know?"

By that time they were driving about two miles an hour down a wooded lane filled with potholes "big enough to sink an elephant," Perdant complained.

"I bet your crazy pacifist pastor talked everyone into it," he said. "Is that it?"

Jules stared at him for a moment, then said, "Maybe people just do what they believe is right."

"How do they think lawlessness is right?"

"Maybe the law is wrong," Jules suggested.

"You can't pick and choose the laws you like or don't like, just willy-nilly." Perdant had been weaving the car around the biggest potholes but couldn't avoid them all, and with a heavy *thunk*, the car's front wheels sank up to their axle in mud.

Perdant tried driving it out of the mudhole and got

nowhere. He tried gunning it. He tried rocking it. He tried backing up. Nothing worked. The car stayed stuck. He rested his head on the steering wheel for a moment.

"I didn't say *like* or *not like*." Jules continued his argument as if they were parked on a shady lane to have a conversation. "I said *right* or *wrong*. Everybody knows what is wrong, but some people are too afraid to say or do anything. And some people manage to do a lot of twisty turns in their minds because they *wish* it to be right. But you can't make it right by *wanting* it to be right."

"You know how to drive . . . *right*?" Perdant said.

Jules knew how to drive a team of horses hitched to a hay wagon. He'd never driven a car. But he'd been watching Perdant drive for more than an hour. How hard could it be?

While Perdant got out and went around the back, Jules climbed into the driver's seat and studied the situation. There were some pedals on the floor and a stick he'd seen Perdant jerking around. Jules yanked on the stick—it made an unpleasant grinding sound.

"You have to put the clutch in when you shift!" Perdant yelled from behind the car.

"Clutch," Jules murmured, looking down at the pedals. Is one of these the clutch? he wondered.

"You know what is the trouble with you people?" Perdant said.

"What?" Jules said, giving each of the pedals a tap with a foot.

"You care more about foreigners than you care about your

own countrymen. You'd let Frenchmen, Frenchwomen, and French children suffer just to help out some hapless foreigners who do not have our country's interests at heart."

"How does helping others make French people suffer?" Jules said.

"Well," Perdant explained, "there are many reasons, most you probably wouldn't understand. But I bet you understand food. You'd let Frenchmen starve so you could feed foreigners—foreigners generally up to no good, I might add."

"Nobody's starving," Jules said, though his stomach was making the same kind of grinding noise the shifter stick had when he moved it. "At least not around here." He was hungry all the time. And at that moment he was as hungry as he'd ever been—he would have eaten pretty much anything right then. Still, he wasn't about to *die* of hunger.

Perdant let out an exasperated puff of air and turned his attention to getting the car unstuck. He hollered at Jules to go forward, backward, rock it, gun it. Once Jules had figured out the pedals and shifter, he tried all those things, sometimes all at once.

The tires spun; mud spattered. The sound of aimlessly spinning tires reminded Perdant of winter, when his car was frequently stuck in the snow.

As he leaned his weight against the car, he could no more stop the thoughts and memories that flung themselves at him than he could stop the mud from spattering his trousers—or the snow that had fallen relentlessly all that winter . . .

What he couldn't help thinking about were his failed arrests. Like that Anton Smelyansky, whom he'd waited for while the cook had offered him a cup of coffee. Waited and waited, and the fellow had never shown up—he must have climbed out a window while Perdant was in the kitchen. While he was waiting, he thought the gendarmes were out arresting people, but later he'd heard that those same gendarmes had talked loudly as they strolled the country roads—shouting back and forth about whom they were going to arrest. Or they told the suspects to pack a bag—they'd be back in a half hour. Of course no one was there when the gendarmes returned.

The bus meant to carry away all the criminals had driven away that day with only two people inside—the brothers Perdant had arrested at the carpentry shop. All the others were like those small, darting trout in the stream one of the boys was able to catch with his bare hands. They slipped out of his grasp, over and over again.

CÉLESTE MEETS UP
WITH JEAN-PAUL

Céleste heard Jean-Paul's jingly, rattly bike before she saw him wheeling it up the long hill to the Mousset farm. She joined him, pushing her own bike alongside.

"Are you ever going to fix that?" she asked.

"Fix what?"

"That rattly jingle," she said. "Or maybe it's a jingly rattle."

"No," Jean-Paul said with a laugh. "I think it frightens Perdant."

"Really?" Céleste asked. "Why?"

Jean-Paul shrugged.

"Where have you been, anyway?" she asked as Jean-Paul held the gate open for her.

"You know better than to ask that," he said.

"I know you weren't on a mission," she guessed.

"Fine." Jean-Paul paused to park his bike outside his room. "I was at the university."

"The university?" Céleste struggled with her kickstand before giving up and leaning her bike against his. "What were you doing there?"

Before Jean-Paul could answer, Mme Mousset called from the house, "Come and get something to eat! Both of you!"

Céleste and Jean-Paul went inside the farmhouse and into the aroma of cooking food and smoked meat. Salamis and hams hung from the ceiling and drying mushrooms dangled from strings like Christmas decorations.

Céleste whispered to Jean-Paul, "What were you doing at the university?"

"Sit! Sit!" Mme Mousset said, standing with two steaming bowls of soup in her hands.

The two of them sat. Mme Mousset set the soup in front of them and pulled up a chair.

"Going to medical school," Jean-Paul said.

Céleste's spoon clattered against her bowl. "Medical school? But . . ."

"Yes, I know," Jean-Paul said. "I made myself a student identity card."

"You enrolled in medical school? But isn't that . . ." Céleste exclaimed, "That's so dangerous!"

"Look," Jean-Paul said. "I'm forbidden to exist, so what difference does it make if I go to forbidden school or not? Or if I forge illegal documents? What should I be afraid of? The risk is the same if I do nothing."

Céleste closed her eyes for a moment at the injustice of it.

"I heard about the raid," Jean-Paul said. "People at the station were talking about it."

"That's why I'm here," Céleste said.

She was about to go on when Monsieur Mousset came into the room. He took off his beret and smoothed the thin threads of his hair with his sunbrowned hand. His face was brown, too, right up to where his cap ended, and his pale, mostly bald head glowed in the dim light.

"Perdant came the other day," M. Mousset said, pulling out a chair from the table and sitting down.

Jean-Paul put down his spoon. "And . . . ?" he said.

"It seemed he was looking for something," the farmer went on.

"Did he find what he was looking for?" Jean-Paul asked, although from the twinkle in his friend's eye, he was quite sure the policeman had not.

"No." M. Mousset chuckled. "Though he looked everywhere. The house, your room, the barn, in the stalls, threw the hay around, turned over stones in the garden, hunted all over. Finally, he took a good, long look at the beehives, until I was certain he would stick his hand right inside one of them. But he thought better of it."

"The beehives . . . ?" Céleste wondered.

"There are two that aren't occupied," M. Mousset explained.

"At least not by bees," Madame Mousset added.

"Well, that's the second close call I've had recently," Jean-Paul said.

"What was the other one?" Céleste asked.

Jean-Paul leaned over his bowl and let the steam clear his

nasal passages. The aroma was so rich, he could smell it through his clogged nose. "I nearly got caught with the papers," he said.

"What?" Céleste said. A spoonful of soup teetered by her mouth, untasted. "Why did you have them with you? You should have dropped them off before you went."

"I know! I know!" Jean-Paul coughed. "Long story."

"Out with it," Céleste said.

Jean-Paul told them the whole story, including being saved by the lozenges. "So you see," he finished, "it was probably good that I stopped at the pharmacy." He pulled out the small tin and set it on the table and tapped the lid with his fingernail. "Those lozenges saved my hide."

"This?" Céleste said, giving the tin a little shake.

Jean-Paul's breath quickened at the sound of it. His heart raced.

"It sounds like cartridges," Céleste said.

"Yeah." Jean-Paul pocketed the tin.

Madame Mousset patted him on the shoulder.

"You've had a good scare," Céleste said, "and I hate to ask, but can you get some identity cards done on the double? Like tonight?" She explained that some of the boys had escaped the raid.

Jean-Paul blew his nose and said, "Where's Jules?"

"Nobody knows." Céleste shrugged.

"He was with Perdant the other day," M. Mousset said.

Céleste and Jean-Paul looked at each other. "Uh-oh," they said simultaneously. "That can't be good."

"When do you have school again?" Céleste asked.

"Not going back," Jean-Paul answered.

"Today was bad luck," Céleste said. "But that doesn't mean you can't go back to school. Just don't bring forged papers with you next time!"

"My student ID is a forged paper!" Jean-Paul protested. Then his shoulders slumped. "It's a risk I don't have to take. And anyway, I have enough work to keep me busy here."

Céleste stared into her bowl. "I'm sorry."

Jean-Paul tipped his head over his soup, letting the steam fog up his glasses. His eyes started to water, and he had to dig in his pocket for his hanky to wipe his nose.

"I'm sorry to ask you to do this," Céleste said. "I'm afraid you've made yourself sick working so hard."

"It's just a cold," Jean-Paul muttered. He knew it wasn't just the cold that had him dabbing at his welling eyes. The stress and fatigue of the long day had taken its toll, but it was also his friend's concern for him, and the kindness of this simple farm family who shared their food, sheltered him, took risks on his behalf, yet asked no questions, expected nothing in return.

After their meal, Jean-Paul and Céleste stepped out of the warm farmhouse into the cool night. Jean-Paul handed over the documents for Max he'd had tucked in his jacket sleeves and said if Jules didn't show up, he'd ride his bike out to the château to deliver the new papers for the others himself.

"I'll get to work on them right now," he said. "I guess it was stupid to try to go to medical school. I've just always wanted to be a doctor."

"Why do you want to be a doctor?" Céleste asked him.

"To save lives!" Jean-Paul said. "Why else do you become a doctor?"

"But, Jean-Paul," Céleste protested. "You *are* saving lives! In that little surgery of yours with your pens and engraving tools laid out like knives and scalpels. You're saving lives every day. And tomorrow it will be Henni's friend Max and the other fellows who need to get out."

"And without any degree at all!" he said with a rueful chuckle.

Maybe in some almost unimaginable future he'd go back to medical school. But for the time being his surgery was right here, and there were a lot of very needy patients.

OUT OF THE MUD

The car lurched out of the mud and onto the dry road, and Perdant's memory, as if released by the snows of winter, skipped to spring.

"I made some arrests," he said to Jules once the car was bumping along again.

"What?" Jules said. "Just now?" He looked behind them, as if he'd missed a crime scene maybe.

"No, this spring," Perdant said, trying to wipe the worst of the mud off the front of his trousers.

"You brought a whole bus," Jules said. "Why a whole bus?"

"We would have needed it if I could have emptied the school of students. If I could have had them all assemble in the town hall and taken a good look at them and their papers. But how do you empty a school when there isn't one? When the classrooms are scattered all over town? Word would quickly spread, and the students would disappear as they seem so good at doing. You need the element of surprise for something like that."

Jules didn't disagree. This was true.

The element of surprise was something Perdant could never seem to get. Somehow the villagers seemed to know what he was going to do before he did it. Before he even knew he was going to do it.

"But I got the brothers," Perdant said.

"Why? What was the point of that?"

"I didn't make the list," Perdant said. "I was just following orders. It's not that I enjoy arresting teenagers."

"Then why do you do it?"

"Somebody has to uphold the law. What if everybody just went around disobeying laws and there was no consequence for it?"

"What law were they breaking? What were they doing wrong?" Jules said.

"You have to obey the law!" Perdant insisted again. He carefully maneuvered through the ruts and potholes until they were back on an actual road.

"They weren't doing anything wrong!" Jules cried.

Perdant didn't really have an answer to that, because the truth was, he'd been fulfilling a quota. After two German officers were killed in Paris, Hitler demanded two thousand French Jews in retribution. The two brothers were part of the quota.

"I'm not a bad person, you know," Perdant said. "I'm just a regular guy. But I have a job. It requires me to do certain things."

"Maybe you should get a different job."

"Ha!" Perdant scoffed. "Like what? Anyway, it's just a job. It's not who I am."

"You are what you do," Jules said.

Perdant looked at Jules, imagining whiskers twitching on his little ferret face. "Who says that?" Perdant grumbled. "*You are what you do.*"

"Nobody has to say it. It just *is*."

"Always with the smart mouth," Perdant said, hoping to shut him up. He was hoping to at last remember one of his successful arrests. He wanted to remember the methodical approach he took in finding the brothers and catching them. He wanted to focus on his triumphant entry into the woodworking shop, the look of fear on the boys' faces. He wanted to think about the moment he burst into the shop and said the line he'd practiced several times in the mirror: "At last, I've got you!"

But what his mind flew to was the clean scent of wood shavings, the sweet smell of sawdust. And the crowd surrounding the bus parked outside the woodworking shop. The two Jewish boys had sat on the bus while other young people came and handed them little gifts. One young boy went onto the bus to give the brothers a rare and precious gift of chocolate.

Why was this what he remembered? And why was it that what stuck in his mind was the song the other students sang:

Must we take leave of one another without hope
Without hope of return?
Must we take leave of one another
Without hope of meeting again one day?

Why was he remembering the teenagers who had laid down in the street in an attempt to prevent the bus from taking the boys away? Why did he remember the sound of the young people's voices singing?

No, we shall meet again, my brothers
It is only a goodbye!
Yes, we shall meet one another again one day
It is only a goodbye.

Why did this, which should seem like a rare success for him, now feel like his biggest failure?

MAX IN THE HAYLOFT

In the hayloft where he'd stayed these last weeks, Max was contemplating hay. As a child he'd loved the barn at his uncle's farm in the German countryside. The smell had meant playing in the hayloft with cousins; it had meant milk fresh from the cow, and brown bread spread with creamy butter. There was a stream nearby with a little waterfall where they swam and bathed, and somehow he had come to associate the sweet, grassy smell of hay even with that.

But later, when he'd been forced to work as unpaid farm labor in one of Hitler's programs in Germany, harvesting hay by day and sleeping in it by night, the stuff got into his hair and clothes, poking and scratching, as unpleasant as the people he'd worked for, until he hoped to never see a stalk of it again.

But when he'd come to Les Lauzes, where had he been hidden? In a hayloft. The smell had come to mean a good night's sleep—not worried that the farmer would turn him in the next day; it meant a bowl of soup in the evening and a soft-boiled egg brought to him by the farmer's kids in the morning. Here his love of hay had been restored, and so had his faith in humanity. Even the dog was on his side, warning him when any stranger came into the farmyard—

As the dog was doing now, in fact—plaintive yowls punctuated by sharp, staccato yips. Max sat up. He eyed the ladder. Would it be best to dash out now? Or wait? He strained to hear past the barking. There was no sound of a car or motorcycle. When the barking stopped, Max heard only the ticking of bicycle wheels, the crunch of footsteps, and a young woman's voice calling to the farmer. "Hello!" she called out. "It's Céleste!"

PERDANT AND JULES ARE STILL NO CLOSER TO THE CHÂTEAU

The road had grown more like an oxcart trail and less like a road and finally ended in a rocky field.

"What is this?" Perdant said between his teeth. "This is not a road! First we go one way, then another, then backtrack . . . We've gone up and down a half dozen little roads, and now we end up here—where there's nothing. I know you know how to get there. You're deliberately misleading me!"

"It's just that I never go anywhere by car!" Jules said. "It's different than striding straight off across the fields. It's so much more complicated when you have to follow roads." He drew little zigzagging motions in the air with his finger to indicate the complexity of it.

Perdant put the car into reverse, jerked it into a three-point turn, then bumped back along the uneven trail until it again transformed into a proper gravel road.

At some point Jules was really going to have to tell the

policeman how to get to the château. *Then* how was he going to prevent him from getting there?

Jules's fingers brushed against the sandpapery sugar lumps in his pocket; he remembered hearing that you could damage a car engine by putting sugar in the gas tank. How much sugar? How long did it take? How could he possibly get these lumps into the tank?

He cleared his throat.

Perdant looked at him.

"Maybe if I get out and take a look around, I'll get my bearings," Jules said. "Also, I gotta . . . Well . . . I drank a lot of tea before we left."

Perdant groaned, pulled over by the side of the road, and shut off the engine. Jules got out and shut the door. Without the puttering of the motor, the quiet of the night was tremendous. It was so big, it was like a thing, Jules sometimes thought. It was like having been swallowed by a gigantic but benevolent monster, and all the stars were its many teeth, the Milky Way its long tongue.

The moon had yet to emerge from behind the hills, but its imminent arrival was heralded by a yellow glow on the eastern horizon.

A perfect night for a parachute drop, Jules thought with disappointment. No matter what happened now, he would miss it. If he kept Perdant busy and out of the way, which was what he should do, he'd miss it. And if he didn't keep Perdant from finding the place, and they ended up at the château, well, then everybody would miss it—and it would be his fault for not keeping Perdant away.

Jules walked to the back of the car, aware of the sound of

his shoes against the gravel, and placed himself facing away from Perdant and the car.

I could just make a run for it, he thought, looking out at the curving hills that disappeared into the darkness. Just take off up and over the hills and disappear.

Sure, Perdant would be pissed off, but so what? Perdant was always sort of pissed off. The policeman's promise to get Jules's dad out of a POW camp? Even if he did have that kind of clout, which he didn't, Jules knew Perdant wasn't going to get Jules's father out of prison, because his father wasn't even *in* prison. He was at that château with a whole bunch of other *maquisards* right now.

And it was up to Jules to make sure Perdant didn't get there.

He tilted his head up toward the big dark vault of the sky and considered the multitude of stars spilled across it. Spilled like sugar in a gas tank, he thought.

He glanced over his shoulder at the car. He could make out Perdant's square shoulders rising above the driver's seat and the back of his head as he looked straight ahead.

There was no way to unscrew the gas cap without him noticing, Jules realized. *No way*. So he stood a while longer, gazing up at the stars and imagining eating a dessert of whipped cream and strawberries, and after a time, he heard a car door slam.

"How much tea did you drink, anyway?" Perdant said. "You've been at it so long that now I gotta go."

Over his shoulder, Jules watched Perdant crossing to the other side of the road. "I hope you know that the friends you probably think you're protecting by leading me on this wild-goose chase are not so innocent," Perdant called over his shoulder. "Some of your friends are engaged in some very serious criminal activity—the kind of lawbreaking that could get them killed!"

"Who?" Jules called to him.

"That redheaded fellow, for one," Perdant said, stopping a short distance in front of the car and turning his back to Jules. "The Scout."

Jules stopped paying attention. He had suddenly realized his opportunity. Not bothering to button his fly, he took the few steps to the back of the car and, crouching, quietly unscrewed the gas cap. He set the cap on the rear bumper, dug in his pockets for the sugar lumps, and fed them into the tank as fast as he could while keeping his eye trained on Perdant's back. When he saw Perdant zipping up, he hotfooted it into the passenger seat. He was sitting idly rolling the window up and down when Perdant got in and slammed the door.

He looked over at Jules and said, "Have you remembered how to get to the château?"

"Yes, I think I have my bearings now," Jules said.

"Good," Perdant said. "Because if there are any more shenanigans, I'll send you to jail, where you belong." He threw the car into gear; it lurched a bit and, toward the back of the car, there was a little *clunk*.

"Did you hear that?" Perdant asked.

"Hear what?"

"That clunk."

"Clunk?" Jules said, remembering the gas cap he'd left on the rear bumper.

"Yes, *clunk*!"

"Probably a rock."

Perdant clenched his jaw but pulled ahead and turned to Jules.

"So, which way?"

Jules pointed behind them.

Once again, Perdant maneuvered the car around on the narrow gravel road and headed back the way they had come. Shortly after they turned around, the front driver's-side tire bumped up and over something, causing the chassis to rock unevenly.

"These roads!" Perdant muttered.

"Terrible, " Jules agreed, wondering what the gas cap looked like now.

TO THE CHÂTEAU

Céleste met Sylvie and her bedraggled group of young men at the gate to the château. When Céleste had met Léon there before, she'd assumed the place had been unoccupied. This time, they were stopped by a voice shouting, "*Halte!*"

A young man Céleste didn't recognize emerged from behind the gate posts. He pointed a rifle at them and demanded a password.

"Put that down!" Sylvie said so sharply that Céleste jumped in surprise. "We want to see the boss."

"Only one," the sentry said. "Which one of you is in charge?"

"She is," Sylvie said, pointing at Céleste.

Céleste started to protest, but the guard took her arm, said, "Come with me," and guided her through the gate, along the gravel drive, and past a small herd of grazing goats. They climbed the stone staircase, still elegant in spite of the moss and wildflowers growing in its many cracks and fissures. Inside, a few lanterns glowed, revealing carved pillars and painted frescoes under the crumbling plaster.

The sentry told her to wait in the foyer while he went outside. Céleste stood for a few moments watching bats performing dizzying acrobatics in the vault of the high ceiling and listening to pigeons cooing in the rafters. The place was clearly not *entirely* uninhabited!

The sound of men's voices—shouts, cheers, laughter—drew her to an open window. Outside, in the almost-darkness, she beheld a bunch of grown men leaping about like schoolboys. What on earth was going on? she wondered, until she noticed the soccer ball being kicked from foot to foot.

Their voices rang like bells against the rocky hill that rose behind the château. The happy sound seemed to come from far away—as if seeping through a crack in the wall of time, a memory from her childhood, or perhaps from some time in the future.

She watched the sentry approach a few of the men and speak for a few moments; then they followed him back to the house. When they entered, she saw that one of them was Léon, wearing a scruffy beard.

"What are you doing here?" he whispered. "You were supposed to bring us a suitcase, not a bunch of kids!"

The suitcase! Céleste had forgotten to retrieve it! "I'll bring it later," she said.

"We might not be here later," Léon said.

"I'll get it to you," Céleste insisted.

One of the older men Céleste recognized as a blacksmith in Les Lauzes approached them. He seemed to be the leader.

"There's been a raid," Céleste said quickly before he could kick her out.

"A raid? Was it Perdant?" asked the blacksmith. His voice echoed in the empty foyer.

"No, it was Germans," she said. "We think Gestapo, but plainclothes, so we don't know for sure."

"Perdant's at fault. He tipped them off," said one of the others.

"I'm not so sure about that . . ." Céleste said. "He didn't seem to know anything about it. Some people say he had warned the house that it might be targeted."

"Because he targeted it," the blacksmith said. "And he's coming after us next."

Céleste remembered what Madame Créneau had said about retribution. She knew she must say something, but her throat felt thick and closed, her mouth dry. She shouldn't be afraid of this man—he was on their side, after all.

"Listen to me," she said, finding her voice. "No retaliation. You're to leave Perdant alone. We can't have anything jeopardize the rescue operation. And you know what could happen if any action is taken against Germans—the SS and Gestapo have demonstrated their willingness to slaughter civilians in retaliation."

"We're aware," the man said, his mouth tight.

Céleste squared her shoulders and planted her feet firmly, looking up at him with her hands on her hips.

The man looked down at her with a slight smirk on his face, which softened into a rather sweet smile and at last broke into a little chuckle. "You're a fierce little tiger, aren't you?"

"Yes," she growled, not smiling. "I am." She hoped he couldn't tell she was trembling. Before her courage gave out she plunged ahead. "A few fellows who escaped need a safe place to stay. I thought they could stay here. I thought it was empty."

"Well, it isn't," one of the men grumbled.

"It's just for a night," she said. "Or two."

"If these boys are being hunted by the Gestapo or any other German outfit," the blacksmith said, "they can't stay around here for long."

"They'll be moved tomorrow," she promised, wondering just how that was going to happen.

PERDANT AND JULES
HAVE CAR TROUBLE

The low-lying spots were foggy enough that Perdant had to put the windshield wipers on going through them. In the fog, he doubted; he lost track of what the point of the trip was, what he was doing. He started to question, and it was getting darker, the long summer twilight fading into night. He had only himself, a gun, and a completely unreliable ten-year-old kid with him. What did he think he was going to accomplish?

Then the car would burst out into the clear evening—landmarks reappeared, the familiar shapes of distant mountains, a dark patch of pines, a field of ripening rye—and his courage returned. His resolve returned. He was capable, he told himself.

But now the car lurched and coughed and sputtered like a stage actor pretending to die of consumption.

Ça y est! Jules thought. That's it! The sugar lumps were working.

He wanted to crow! To howl with glee! But he didn't. He sat on his hands and bit his lip.

Perdant cursed. "Come on . . ." he muttered. He urged the car forward by rocking a little, as if that would keep it moving.

Finally, on an upward rise, the car coughed itself into silence. Jules sat for a moment in smug satisfaction of a job well done. Then he noticed the gas gauge, the needle on empty.

"We've run out of petrol," Jules said, wishing he had those sugar lumps back. He was so hungry! Even one would be something.

"That thing is busted," Perdant said. "Been busted since I got this car. On the other hand, we've been driving around in the hinterlands so long that we probably *have* run out of gas!" He got out, slammed the door, went around to the front, and opened the hood.

Jules told himself he should stop thinking about the sugar and think about what came next. Would Perdant give up now and just walk back to the village and go to bed? That would be the best-case scenario. So it probably wouldn't happen like that. Perdant seemed so all-fired intent on getting to the château, he'd probably walk there, Jules supposed.

Here's how it will go, he thought. Perdant will say, "Come on, let's walk." Then he'll reach in and get his gun—his gun that's in the glove box.

Keeping his gaze fixed on the hood, which was still obscuring the windshield, Jules gently opened the glove box, slowly reached in, and without taking his eyes off the hood of the car, felt for Perdant's pistol—it was as he remembered it, barrel facing toward the passenger side, stock facing the driver's side. It was warm from the engine and heavier than he expected as he slipped it into his jacket pocket.

With any luck, he thought, as the hood of the car slammed down, he wouldn't shoot his own foot off.

"I don't think it's much of a walk back to the village," Jules said as he climbed out of the car. "I can show you the fast way. And we can try for the château tomorrow."

"Oh, no," Perdant said. "No, no. I'm not quitting now. I know you."

Even in the darkness, Jules could see Perdant's pale finger stabbing the air at him. "If we wait 'til tomorrow, there'll be nobody there. You know very well where this place is, and you are going to take me there—*now*. Even if we have to go on foot. Which it looks like we will."

Perdant stepped around to the passenger side, opened the door, reached into the glove box, opened it, groped around inside, and muttered, "Didn't I put my sidearm in there? I usually put my gun there."

He started a frantic search under the front seat, then in the back, until he stopped and pointed at Jules. "La Crapule," he said. "You scoundrel! Give me the pistol."

Perdant lunged at Jules, but Jules had learned a thing or two from his goats about dodging, feinting, and other sneaky maneuvers.

He dodged Perdant, then dashed out into the field.

Perdant gave chase as Jules zigzagged through the grass. "You little rascal!" the policeman hollered, but he had to give up calling him names when he ran out of breath. Eventually, he had to stop chasing him altogether and bent over with his hands on his knees, gasping.

"Scoundrel!" he sputtered at the small shadowy figure in the field.

"It's for your own safety," Jules called to Perdant from a distance. "If you're right about that château being full of *maquisards*."

"That was your idea, not mine," Perdant said, panting. "I never said anything about *maquisards*."

"Well, what if it is?" Jules said. "If you go in armed and the place is full of them: *Boom*. You're dead. If you go in without a gun, they probably won't shoot you, at least not right off the bat. I can't promise that, but it's better than the alternative."

"So you're suddenly worried about my safety?" Perdant said, standing up, his chest still heaving.

Jules didn't answer, but the truth was, he didn't want them to kill Perdant.

"Well, doesn't matter," Perdant said, breathing heavily. "The police are on their way . . . Several cars' worth . . . Bringing a truck, probably. I'm sure they'll have no trouble locating the château without my help. Who knows what they'll do to whomever they find there. Maybe if I was there, I could plead for leniency—at least for any locals who might get caught up in their sweep."

The two of them stood staring at each other, but in the dark they couldn't see each other's eyes, and neither one could tell if the other was bluffing.

PHILIPPE IS *GRILLÉ*

Philippe woke in that way you do when you feel first what's in your heart before your head takes over, and what he felt at the core of his being was that he'd come home. Though he was far away from Normandy, he realized that it was here where he felt most at home—here in this slightly ratty chair, its arms shredded from cats' claws and its cushion saggy from supporting the weight of so many forlorn visitors.

Madame Créneau had returned from her little junket with Henni and Madeleine to find Philippe asleep in her one upholstered chair. And he woke to see her sitting in a small circle of light, pulling apart an old sweater—he supposed so she could reknit it into something one of the children could wear.

It was as if his mother sat across from him, not exactly knitting, but instead *unknitting* a sweater. Soon she would look up, smile, exchange a few pleasantries, give him something to eat, and tell him about the next group he was to shepherd over the border to Switzerland. But when he remembered all that had transpired, he slumped back into the chair.

"I am *grillé*," he pouted. "Done. Finished. Now that the police know who I am and what I do, I can no longer do this work."

"Yes, I heard about your arrest," Madame said. "Thank goodness you were released. Maybe your youthful looks helped. They could hardly hold a child!"

Philippe made a goofy face and said, "They let the nurse go, too."

"Good," Madame said, adding, "Put your hands out like this."

"Are you going to slap my hands?" he asked, sticking his arms straight out in front of him.

She chuckled and began to loop the yarn around his wrists. "No. But, yes, you are *grillé*," she agreed. "You are done."

"Done?" He had expected her to say, "Oh, you can go a different route." Or something along those lines. Not to tell him he was "done"! Without this work . . . what would he do?

"We'll find something for you to do," she said, winding ever more yarn around his arms. "Look how useful you're being now!"

Philippe looked down at the yarn around his arms. Like soft, fuzzy handcuffs, he thought.

"Listen," Mme Créneau said, "you can't live on adrenaline forever."

"What do you mean?"

"You'll burn yourself into a cinder. Life is not one long rush of adrenaline. Which seems like what you're trying to make it. It would be wise if you could learn to enjoy life as it comes—a more normal life."

"Is there such a thing in these times?" Philippe asked, adding, "I'm not trying to be cheeky."

She tilted her head, acknowledging the truth of the question. "Perhaps you'd be wise to apply yourself to your schoolwork."

"School!" he exclaimed. "That's the most boring of all!"

"Don't you sometimes just long for 'boring'? Just regular, boring life? The thought of it is so appealing to me, I can't tell you."

He looked at her, noticing for the first time the fatigue on her face, the dark circles under her eyes.

"Isn't this what we're fighting for?" she went on. "To be allowed to go back to our old, boring lives? To be allowed to go to school in peace? To learn about all kinds of things that challenge us, challenge our intellect? Our long-held beliefs? What we think we know?"

He'd never thought of school like that, but he supposed in the study of so many things—philosophy, religion, history, maybe even math and science—there were things that would make him think in new ways.

"Okay, I'll go back to school," he said.

"Well"—Madame slipped the skein of yarn off his wrists—"not *quite* yet."

"Another assignment?" he asked, feeling the familiar champagne-like fizz of excitement in his stomach.

"There's been a raid. A bad one. And there are some students who need to get out."

"How do you propose I do that?"

"That, my dear boy, is exactly what you have to figure out. And figure it out fast, because they need to be moved tomorrow."

JULES AND PERDANT MAKE A STOP

Jules was now trying to blame their inability to find the château on some supernatural thing he called the Triangle de la Burle, a triangle-shaped area between three local mountains.

"Strange, unexplained things happen inside the triangle," Jules said. "And the thing is, Château de Roque is right in the middle of it. It could be that the château appears and disappears, and right now it's just not there, and that's why we can't find it."

"That is the most ridiculous thing I've ever heard," Perdant said.

"No, but it's true. All kinds of weird things happen inside the triangle. There was a man who got lost in there and showed up years later, having no idea how much time had passed. Another time an airplane crashed for no reason. I can show you where," Jules said.

"No thanks."

Perdant quit listening. He'd let the scoundrel have the gun—if he even had it, which he doubted. Probably Perdant hadn't brought it. Now he couldn't remember.

Jules quit talking, too, and they walked in silence until Perdant said, "*Mon Dieu*, I'm starving."

"Me too," Jules agreed.

"Do you have any food tucked away in that voluminous jacket?"

Jules dug around in his pockets and pulled out a lump of something coated with grit, sand, pocket fluff, and pine needles. He offered it to Perdant.

"That is disgusting," Perdant said, making a face. "What is it?"

"Cheese?" Jules guessed. He picked off the worst of the outer coating and nibbled at it. "Goat cheese, I think."

"No thanks," Perdant said. "Let's stop at that farm." He pointed to a nearby farmhouse. "It looks like they're still up. There's a light in their window. Maybe they have a telephone."

Jules said nothing, silently following Perdant up the trail to the house.

A dog barked its head off. Naturally. Every farm had a barking dog, Perdant had long since realized. A ready-made alarm system.

The dog seemed to know Jules, though, and wagged its tail and pressed its head against Jules's leg.

The farmer and his wife were awake. Still dressed, even.

"Late hours for a farmer," Perdant observed. He also noticed that the farmer moved the lantern from the window to the kitchen table, but he didn't mention it.

"I don't suppose you have a telephone?" Perdant asked.

No, of course they didn't.

"A glass of wine?" the farmer offered.

"Some *quatre-quart?*" the farmwife added.

Perdant and Jules brightened at the thought of the rich pound cake, made with lots of eggs and butter—the kind of thing you only got at a farm where there were chickens and a cow.

They pulled up chairs to the table, where they were each served a generous slice of cake. Perdant was given a small tumbler of wine, and Jules got one of milk.

The cake was so delicious, and Jules was so hungry, that he momentarily forgot to pay attention to the conversation. When he tuned back in, he was alarmed to hear Perdant saying, ". . . sure you haven't had any compulsory-labor dodgers or anti-patriots come around here?"

The farmer shook his head.

"What about Jews?" Perdant said. "Seen any Jews?"

Jules lifted his head. What a rude question to ask someone who was feeding you cake, he thought.

"I don't know . . ." the farmer said. "What do they look like?"

Perdant abandoned this line of questioning and gave himself over to his cake, chewing without further comment.

Jules knew Perdant was a little hard of hearing, but he wasn't sure he was so deaf that he couldn't hear the shuffling of shoes on the floor above, and the tiny mouselike scraping sound of coat hangers on a closet rack.

»» ««

Upstairs, Henni and Madeleine were as far back in the closet as they could get, wrapped in the farmer's coats, with their feet in his boots.

The shearling coat in which Henni was hiding tickled her nose, and although she clamped her lips together and quietly slid her hand over her mouth, still, she convulsed in a sneeze. Stifled, but audible. Afterward, she held her breath, listening for footsteps on the stairs.

Instead, she heard chairs scrape against the floor, the sound of something being poured into glasses, low voices speaking French—Henni couldn't catch the murmured words.

Then, clearly, she heard the policeman say, ". . . seen any Jews?"

If there was an answer to that, Henni didn't hear it, the words covered by the steady ticking of the grandfather clock at the bottom of the stairs. She thought of Max. She wished she could warn him that the policeman was out prowling. She imagined going to visit him at the château where Céleste had taken him.

She knew that château. She had seen it on one of the first days she'd been in Les Lauzes. She and others from the Beehive had been sent to help harvest apples.

"When you are finished with your task, you can eat," they'd been told. Whereupon all the kids shimmied right up into the trees and immediately started stuffing themselves with fruit.

From her vantage point in the tree, Henni could see the world—or this world, anyway: beyond the orchards, the fields, their haystacks glowing golden in the sun; the lazy cows, flicking their ears against the flies; the hay wagons trundling along, pulled by gentle oxen; the hazy distance . . . Somewhere, in some other village, every windowpane was rattling from the steady thud of explosions, howling sirens, the wailing of children. All over, the war raged on. Here, on nearly every farm, in houses and churches and schools and shops, all over the plateau, people were waging a different kind of war. A kind of secret war.

Henni's eyes traced farm fields, windbreaks, farmhouses, barns, and on a far-off hill, the tumbledown ruins of a long-ago castle.

What had happened to the people who had lived in that old château? Had they, like she, been swept away by forces beyond their control?

Remembering the place, she once again thought of Max, sheltering there. She imagined their hands clasping, then too quickly sliding apart. "Remember to stay alive," she wanted to tell him. Then, wrapping the coat around her and Madeleine, she dreamed a coat of protection around him, and over all the children hidden on the mountain.

IN THE LIGHT OF THE MOON

For a long time after the soccer game everyone sat on rocks or in the grass behind the château, watching the moon rise from behind the distant peaks.

Someone had picked a basket of wild plums; leeks and onions had been found in the overgrown garden. There were loaves of rye bread and a large wheel of cheese.

This was all shared, and in the midst of it, Max felt something like fingers brush the back of his neck. He turned, but no one was there. It must be the breeze, he thought, a breeze that proceeded to whisper in his ear. He sometimes thought he heard Henni's low, serious voice, reminding him to stay alive.

"I plan on it," he answered. He almost felt her hands on his—they rested there just a moment before the cool night air lifted the warmth from his fingertips.

Céleste and Sylvie sat together, watching the night creep in, feeling the warmth of the day dissipating. Except for a song thrush repeating its trilling verse over and over, and the occasional wild warble of a nightingale, it was quiet.

"Do you ever wonder . . . ?" Sylvie said. "We have spent so much time doing things that in any other time would be wrong: forging papers, smuggling people, money, contraband, documents . . . When the war is over and peace returns, will we be able to tell right from wrong?"

Céleste couldn't answer. This day! she thought. It was as if all the years of the war had been encapsulated into it: the horror, the cruelty, the sorrow, the arbitrariness of it all. Why that house and not another? Why some people but not others?

She looked around at the *maquisards*, their faces dark silhouettes against the moon. Here and there a button or a watch face glinted in the moonlight. They are waiting for something, Céleste thought. What?

While they waited, the *maquisards* were discussing unfair Vichy and German policies. Léon couldn't resist a joke. "The German barter system works great!" he said. "We give them our wheat, and they take our coal."

There were some chuckles, and Léon leaned over to Céleste and whispered, "The suitcase?"

"I'll get it," she said, rising to go.

AT THE FARM

Jules said something to the farmwife in the local patois, and Perdant reminded him to "speak in French."

"He only asked if he could have another piece of cake," the woman said. She plopped a large slice onto a plate and, with a smile and a wink, slid it across the table to Jules.

Jules tucked in and, trying to cover any sound that might be coming from upstairs, chewed as noisily as he could, smacking his lips and uttering little sounds of pleasure. He fidgeted in his seat, making the old wood chair squeak. He let his knife and fork clatter against the plate, too.

When Perdant gave him a sidelong glance, he toned it down a bit.

Perdant finished his cake, refused a second slice, and got up. "Now," he said, "if you could tell me where Château de Roque is located, I would be obliged."

The farmer's eyes and Jules's met briefly.

"But, why?" the farmer asked. "It's abandoned. No one lives there."

"Nevertheless," Perdant said.

"Well," said the farmer, "it can be hard to find in the dark."

"Just give me directions and we can manage," Perdant said.

"Next road on the right, turn up, then take the first left for one or two kilometers."

"Oh," said the farmer's wife. "I think it's the second left."

"Is it? Or is it a right turn that then goes left?" the farmer said.

When it was clear the conversation was going to continue in this vein, Perdant pulled Jules outside, leaving the farm couple still arguing over the directions with each other.

"Well, at least we got something to eat," said Perdant, and he let out something that sounded almost like a giggle.

This surprised Jules, but he felt it, too, the kind of relief that comes after a tense situation that could have gone badly but didn't. He felt light. Laughter bubbled out of him.

"I'm not totally deaf, you know," Perdant said.

"Eh?" Jules said. "What did you say?"

This wisecrack made Perdant guffaw, and the two of them strolled back down the road into the night, laughing like idiots.

THE YELLOW SUITCASE
IS OPENED

Céleste dragged herself up the stairs to her bedroom, her mind already wrapping itself around her pillow, the desire to collapse into bed almost overwhelming. But then there, under her bed, the yellow suitcase—the suitcase she had promised to bring to the *maquisards*. So she quietly pulled it out from under the bed, tiptoed back down the stairs, and opened the door.

She was surprised to see Philippe coming up the walk, brushing his hand along the tops of the peonies.

"Philippe!" Céleste exclaimed, holding the door open for him. "I can't believe it!"

He stepped inside, and she pulled him into the small dining room and shut the door. "I heard you were arrested," she whispered.

"Guess they decided I was too young to bother with," he said.

She reached out and gingerly touched his black eye. "Looks like someone bothered with you."

He gave a little shrug. "It could have been a lot worse," he said. "Listen, do you know how to sew?"

"Yes, of course," she said. "Or I wouldn't have anything to wear!"

That explained how she always managed to look so stylish, Philippe thought, even these days when clothes were hard to come by. He'd always assumed her parents could afford black-market clothing and had things shipped from Paris. Maybe she didn't live in such impossibly rarified air as he'd thought.

"I wonder if I could enlist your help," he said.

Céleste raised an eyebrow. "Possibly . . . What do you need?"

"Do you think you could sew a bunch of Scout uniforms in a hurry?"

"How much of a hurry?"

"Before daybreak?"

"Philippe!" she exclaimed, laughing. "It's almost daybreak now!"

"I've managed to scrounge . . ." Philippe mumbled as he began to pull items out of his rucksack. "Khaki shorts, berets, kerchiefs. What I'm short on is shirts. But Madame Créneau gave me some parachute silk—" He looked up into her incredulous face. "Come on!" he said. "Get your sewing things and let's go! It'll be an adventure!"

Céleste thought perhaps she'd had enough adventure for one night. On the other hand, maybe she could learn more about this mysterious daredevil. Maybe some of his fearless-ness would rub off on her.

"Where are we going?" she asked.

"You know Château de Roque?"

Céleste laughed and, putting two and two together, said, "Ohhh . . ."

She left the room, returning a moment later with a sewing basket over one arm and the suitcase in the other hand.

"Let me carry that," Philippe said, reaching for the suitcase.

She hesitated before giving it to him.

"There's not a bomb in here, is there?" he asked, holding it to his ear.

"I hope not!" Céleste said. "I don't know. I don't dare open it!"

"Should we look? Aren't you curious?"

They stared at the suitcase. Then Céleste nodded. With Philippe here she felt braver.

Philippe set the suitcase down and flipped open the fasteners. With his hands on the top, he looked up at Céleste.

"Ready?" he said.

"Yes! Open it!" she whispered.

He opened the case, and the two stared in disbelief at the contents.

"Just like Christmas!" Philippe whispered.

"Just what we always wanted," Céleste agreed, ogling the stack of rumpled khaki shirts.

"What else is in there?" Philippe asked.

They rummaged through the contents. "Soap. Medical supplies. Bandages," Céleste said.

"This is meant for the *maquis*," Philippe said, eyeing Céleste.

Céleste tried to look innocent. "I think it's okay if a few shirts go to our Scouts, don't you?" she said. "It's an emergency."

Philippe snapped the suitcase shut and picked it up, and the two of them crept outside, shutting the door quietly behind them.

"I saw you, you know," he said as they walked toward the street. "You and your suitcase."

She tilted her head to look at him. "Yes," she said. Of course, she'd seen him, too.

"This suitcase"—he paused to hold it out so they could regard it—"was the reason I was arrested."

"What? How?"

"I was so worried about what you were carrying in this thing, I didn't pay attention, and I got caught. So I would like to ask you, for my sake, not to go on any more missions."

"Maybe it's *you* who shouldn't go on any more missions," she said. "Anyway, aren't we on one now?"

He laughed. "I guess you're right. It's so pleasant, though, it seems almost like a date."

Céleste ducked her head, hoping that in the darkness he couldn't tell she was blushing. Then, in a rush, before her courage gave out, and to change the subject, she asked, "How do you do what you do? I mean, you must be fearless."

"Fearless?" Philippe said. "No. I'm afraid all the time—I think you have to be. But I guess I kind of enjoy it. It makes me feel, I don't know, *alive*."

"Being afraid just . . . scares me to death!" Céleste said.

They veered from the streets onto a forest path, walking so close, Céleste's arm brushed against his. It felt as if tiny sparks ignited along her arm, and she remembered thinking how he reminded her of a smoldering fire.

"Why *do* you do it?" Céleste asked him.

"I like the work; I'm glad I can help people," he said, smiling. "Sometimes there's even a little money in it. But I guess mainly it's selfish. Although I tell myself I am rescuing some other poor soul, in some way it's my *own* poor soul I'm rescuing."

She grabbed his hand with her free hand. "Yes! I know exactly what you mean," she said. Embarrassed, she started to pull her hand away, but he held on to it. So they continued to walk, hand in hand. "For a long time I watched you and others doing things, and I admired you," Céleste said, "but I was too afraid. I didn't think I could do it—I was sure I'd mess up. Then I went on a little mission. I was still afraid, but I was doing something. I had a little power. I could actually do something to resist. To fight back. And the oddest thing happened. That huge dark fear of what could happen—it went away." She let go of his hand to demonstrate how her fear had wafted away into the night. "I guess I had to do the thing I dreaded most in order to lose my fear of doing it."

Philippe nodded.

"But . . . " she went on. "But today, it feels like everything is unraveling, coming apart. We're losing. They're winning. They're closing in. We're not safe anymore. Nobody's safe."

Philippe tried to think of something to say. He couldn't say she was wrong, because she wasn't. How do you live day in, day out with the danger of just living? Maybe he'd been able to do what he did because his danger had been temporary. As soon as he got back to Sunnyside, he fell asleep, confident in his own safety. Was that no longer true? How would they live with this new fear?

"They're not winning, though," he said to console her—and maybe himself. "The Allies are making progress. The Germans have lost Stalingrad; they're losing in Russia. The Allies are beating Rommel in Tunisia. The Greek liberation army has taken back a city in Greece . . ."

"That's all so far away!" Céleste cried. "It's as if we're fighting our own little war, all by ourselves. And, I don't know. I did something, but was it important? Shirts and soap and bandages? Not exactly saving any lives!"

"It's all important," Philippe said, taking her hand again. "You never know how important the little things turn out to be. I mean, the shirts! That's a little miracle right there!" He flashed her a brilliant smile. "Those shirts are going to get those boys to Switzerland!"

They followed the small trail that led along the rocky hill behind the château, then came around the front, where the guard stopped them. Recognizing them, he let them pass.

The windows had been shuttered so no light shone out, and everything seemed quiet. But when the two friends stepped inside, it was almost as if there'd been a party. Someone was playing a guitar. The heel of a loaf of bread, crumbs of cheese, and dirty glasses rested along the windowsills. The *maquisards* were shouldering their rucksacks and donning their caps and berets, getting ready to go.

Coming from one room, there was a whirring sound like a bicycle and the crackling of static. Céleste peeked in to see a young man pedaling a bicycle missing its wheels, a bicycle that was hooked up to a generator that was connected to a radio transmitter inside a suitcase. Hunched over the transmitter, her eyes narrowed in concentration, was a sharp-featured woman Céleste had never seen before.

The woman slid off her headset and said in bad French with a thick American accent, "Could everyone please be quiet for a moment?"

The place went silent.

Who is that? Céleste mouthed to Philippe.

He shook his head. *Maybe better if we don't know*, he mouthed back.

They tiptoed to another room, where Max and the other young men were resting on blankets rolled out on the floor, playing cards or reading magazines.

"Here are your Scouts, Monsieur," Céleste said by way of introduction.

The suitcase was opened, and shirts and shorts were tried on. Céleste, now beyond fatigue, took out her scissors, a spool of thread, pins, and a sewing needle, and set to work making alterations.

JULES TAKES A STAND

Light was starting to show along the eastern horizon, the crickets had fallen silent, and the breeze had completely died. It was as still as it ever was. The only sound was the crunch of Perdant's and Jules's footsteps, the raspy crowing of a very far-off rooster, and the lowing of cows, even farther away.

For a time Perdant thought he heard voices—like a boy and a girl having a conversation—but then he noticed there was a stream nearby, and the sound must have been water running over stones.

And then there was that strange, yet familiar, jingling—a sound like that of the ghostly dragoon astride a running horse, his spurs jingling. He could have sworn the sound was moving toward him, growing closer and closer. Of course he knew it wasn't, but he looked around anyway, seeing nothing.

But wait, he thought. Not nothing. In the distance, rising out of the early-morning mist, a steep-pitched roof sprouting multiple chimneys, and on one side, a vine-covered turret.

Unless what he was seeing was an illusion created by the Triangle de la Burle, it was a château. *The* château.

He laughed and said, "Finally."

Jules's head snapped up. *Zut alors!* he almost said out loud. He hadn't been paying enough attention! Somehow they'd gotten on the road leading straight to the château. *Now* how was he going to prevent the man from getting there?

"I don't think you should go," he said, putting his hand on Perdant's arm.

"Well, that's been obvious from the beginning," Perdant said, continuing on.

Jules ran after him, grabbed his arm, and tugged. "What if the place is full of *maquisards*?" he pleaded. If Perdant went to the château, the *maquisards* would have to kill him, wouldn't they? What other option was there? Perdant would have seen them all and would know exactly who was involved. They wouldn't be able to just let him go! "It's not—" Jules hesitated. "It might not be safe!"

"You're right," Perdant said. "So you stay here. Or better yet, go home." The policeman kept walking, picking up speed while Jules stayed where he was.

"Stop!" Jules cried.

But the policeman did not stop, not even glancing back when he yelled, "Go home!"

But then Jules shouted, "Stop or I'll shoot!"

Perdant stopped and slowly turned around to see the boy holding his service pistol with both hands. "*Doucement*," Perdant said, taking a stumbling step back. "Take it easy." Recovering, he said in his policeman voice, "You've got no business with that weapon."

"Don't think I don't know how to use this," Jules said, flipping back the safety on the gun. It wasn't so dark that Perdant couldn't tell what he was doing.

"I know, I know. You're a farm kid." Perdant took a hesitant step toward Jules. "Maybe you hunted rabbits with your dad. But this is different."

Jules resisted the temptation to tell Perdant that his dad was probably sorting through canisters of submachine guns about now.

Perdant tried taking another step closer, and Jules took a step back. Emboldened, Perdant moved toward Jules. "Come on, kid," he said in a cajoling tone. "You're not going to shoot me. At least not on purpose."

Perdant was right, but Jules was not about to let him know that, so he held his ground, pointing the pistol with both hands at the policeman's chest. Perdant stopped his approach, and the two of them stood face-to-face for what seemed like an eternity. If that's what it takes, Jules thought, that's what I'll do: hold the man here all day. By then, the *maquisards* will surely be gone, or someone will come by, or something will happen.

But already his arms were tired—the gun was heavy! His wrists wanted to droop.

"Why don't you just tell me what's going on in the château?" Perdant said.

"I'm the one with the gun. I'll be asking the questions," Jules answered. He'd heard that line on a radio show, but never in his life thought he'd ever get to say it. Nor did he think he would ever say *Stop or I'll shoot* in real life. But he didn't like it as much as he would have thought. He would have given anything not to be in this predicament right now, but he didn't know how to get out of it.

He waved the gun a little bit and said, "*You* should be giving *me* some answers. How about you tell me why you want to go to the château? Why there?"

"Why anywhere?" Perdant said.

"Yeah, why anywhere? Why don't you just leave it alone? What do you think you're accomplishing with your spying and hunting and prying and arresting people? Why do you want to do that?"

Why? Perdant wondered. He had posed the same question to himself just the day before. Now he tried to rouse himself to answer with his usual patriotic fervor—to save France for the Frenchmen, save the country from anti-patriots, communists, immigrants, the Jews who had been working to undermine the civilized nations of Europe . . .

The problem was, he wasn't sure he believed it anymore. He slumped against a tree, exhausted by it all. He felt a thought starting at the back of his mind, an idea. As if a lamp had been lit in the far reaches, but its light had not yet penetrated the mass of his brain. He squeezed his forehead between his hands, trying to open a pathway for it. When he looked up, Jules was adjusting his hands on the pistol, his eyes cast down, the gun lowered.

Perdant's mind shifted to the moment at hand. Now! was the thought that muscled past the slow-moving one and propelled

Perdant forward. He leaped on Jules, his intention being to wrest the weapon out of the boy's hands before something stupid happened. But it was harder than he thought it would be. The kid struggled, kicked, lashed out—and did not let go of the gun. If the gun went off, Perdant wondered, which one of them would be hit?

THE GUNSHOT

Philippe was mentally hiking the route he planned to take with his new troop of Scouts: *Into the forest behind the château, across the fields, down the mountain until connecting with the road through*—when his thoughts were interrupted by the sound of a gunshot.

At the sound, Céleste froze, her hand extended to receive the note Max was about to give her. Max's hand stayed outstretched, too, the note for Henni still in it. It was as if a spell had been cast and everyone in the castle had been turned to stone.

But only for an instant. Then the note was passed, the boys began to whisper, and Philippe crossed to the window and opened the wooden shutters. In the thin light of predawn there was little to see except the shimmering of hundreds of dew-wet spiderwebs draped over the fields.

"Keep away from the window," someone whispered.

"The shot wasn't that close," he said, then added "Shh," trying to listen.

The sound of a suitcase snapping shut in the other room seemed as loud as gunfire.

"We should get going," Philippe said, turning away from the window.

"What about our papers?" Max said. "We shouldn't go without papers."

Philippe tapped his foot, trying to decide what to do. His immediate response was the urge to *get out*. To move away from whatever was happening outside. On the other hand, for these young men to travel without false papers could be even more dangerous. It was probably inevitable that they'd be asked to produce identification, especially once they were on the train.

➤➤ ◄◄

Jean-Paul had been pedaling up to the château when he heard the gunshot. He leaped off his bicycle, hoisted it onto his shoulder, and climbed the steps as fast as he could.

Inside, he leaned the bike against a pillar and barely had a moment to take a look around the foyer before Céleste appeared with a sewing basket over her arm. "You've shown up in the nick of time," she said. "They're on hot coals waiting for you."

He followed her while craning his neck to look at everything they passed. "I've never been inside before," he murmured, ogling the high ceiling with its thick wood beams, the marble pillars, the still-graceful archways and tall windows. "Even under the ruin, it's still pretty elegant."

"Kind of like France?" Céleste said.

"Yeah, I guess," he said, still trying to take it all in. "I wonder what it would take to fix it up."

A woman with a suitcase strapped to her back emerged

from another room. "You young people are going to have to do it," she said, "when the time comes." With her long skirt swishing, she turned and walked, limping slightly, down the corridor toward the back entrance.

"Who was that?" Jean-Paul wondered.

Céleste watched the woman's form dissolving into the shadowy corridor. "I don't know, but I think we should soon follow her out. The *maquisards* left earlier."

"We all need to get out as soon as we can," Jean-Paul agreed.

"But first," Céleste gestured down the corridor as she said, "your presence is desired in here."

He followed her, marveling at the way she strode along—as if she had shed her shy girlhood in a single evening. She disappeared around a corner . . . and into adulthood, Jean-Paul mused.

When Jean-Paul stepped into the room after her, he almost burst out laughing. Dressed in khaki shorts and shirts, each with a beret on his head and a kerchief tied around his neck, the young men looked every inch like a Scout troop ready for a hike across the plateau. No doubt that was exactly what they were about to do just as soon as he gave them their new documents.

Jean-Paul passed these out while Philippe waited at the window, mentally finishing the route. Once Philippe had seen the Scouts off on the train with their next guide, he'd board *La Tortue* back to Les Lauzes and sleep all the way home. Then he planned to pay a call on Céleste, gathering a bouquet of daisies and periwinkles as he went. There were many different kinds of thrills in this life, he thought. And perhaps it would not be so boring after all to spend a little more time in the village.

As he looked around at the apprehensive yet hopeful faces of the young men he would soon be guiding, he couldn't help but sing a bit of the Swiss hiking song he intended to teach them along the way.

It's so simple to love
To smile at life . . .
To allow our hearts
To crack the window
To the sun coming in . . .

THE CHÂTEAU'S SECRET

"Hang on, hang on, hang on . . ." Perdant mumbled, staggering under the weight of the boy in his arms. The château loomed ahead, rising out of the mist.

The boy's face was ashen, but he didn't cry. He pressed his hands over the wound in his chest, but blood oozed through his fingers, soaked both their shirts, ran onto the ground. So much blood, Perdant thought. Too much.

What if no one is there? he wondered. Then again, what if the place is full of *maquisards*? Then again, wasn't that what he was counting on—that there might be someone with medical training? Maybe they would miraculously have medical supplies, even though the Germans requisitioned that sort of thing for themselves.

Perdant pushed open the gate, stumbled down the gravel drive, and paused at the bottom of the wide stairs, gasping. He'd been running, and now he was spent. His legs ached; his heart felt sodden and heavy.

Still, he managed to heave both himself and the boy up the first step. Then the next.

On the third Perdant heard the distant growl of cars and the rumble of motorcycles winding their way up to the plateau from the valley. He had forgotten about his earlier call to police headquarters. He glanced at the boy, whose eyes were squeezed shut against the pain.

"Hang on," he said, taking another step.

At last he reached the top and stopped in front of the doors, breathing heavily.

Beyond his own and Jules's labored breaths, it seemed silent. Yet there was something. A whisper of movement, of doors opening and closing, hushed footfalls, quiet voices.

He no longer knew what he did or didn't hear. What he believed or didn't believe. He only knew what he had to do now at this moment, and so he reached for the iron ring that served as a door handle.

"Don't," Jules said, or perhaps the word only lingered in his mind.

But Perdant did.

Perdant had not expected Scouts, but there they were—a whole troop of them, lifting Jules from Perdant's arms, laying him on a table, fetching water, ripping up old shirts. One of them—the redheaded kid—was using the torn shirts to compress the wound in Jules's chest, and another lad—Jean-Paul Filon, whom Perdant had once given a ticket—was assessing the damage.

"Heart wasn't hit," he was saying. "Luckily the bullet penetrated the right side of his chest." Jean-Paul listened through a rolled up magazine to Jules's chest and said, "He seems to be breathing all right, so I don't think the lung has collapsed. Probably broke a rib, though . . ."

"He's lost a lot of blood," Céleste whispered.

"He should be stitched up by a doctor," Jean-Paul said. "But first we need to clean the wound and try to control the bleeding. I don't suppose there's any soap or clean bandages or anything useful like that to be had."

Céleste squeaked and ran for the suitcase.

"As it happens . . ." Philippe began, but he was interrupted when a bowl of clean water was carried in by one of the Scouts.

Céleste returned with the suitcase, threw it down, flung it open, and emerged triumphantly with a bar of soap, antiseptic, and rolls of sterile bandages.

Philippe caught her eye. "Turns out that suitcase was pretty important," he said.

She was just so grateful, she couldn't reply. Soapy water, a clean cloth, Jean-Paul's steady hands and strong nerves. Everything so strangely perfect. There was something almost holy going on.

"There wasn't any suture thread or anything like that in the suitcase," she said to Jean-Paul, "but when it comes to it, I have silk thread and needle. You can sew him up, can't you?"

Jean-Paul didn't have time for the bitterness he might have felt at this moment. Had he been attending medical school as he'd wished, he'd be much better prepared for a situation like this. He'd know for sure if Jules's lung had been hit, probably. But he thought he could stitch him up if he had to. "When it comes to it," he said.

Céleste wet a cloth and pressed it to Jules's forehead. "Hey, Superman," she whispered, remembering what he'd called himself. "You're stronger than steel, remember?"

But not faster than a speeding bullet, Jules tried to say. Wanted to say. It would make them laugh, he thought. But the words wouldn't come. They were there in his mind but couldn't reach his mouth somehow.

"Keep breathing, tiger," Jean-Paul whispered as he washed the blood from the boy's chest. "Your mama's got a lamp burning in the window." He thought of how the boy had come to him just when he'd needed him, somehow unbidden—like an angel, sort of. A strange, scoundrelly angel.

Some of the Scouts peeled the paper wrapping off bandages and handed them to Philippe, who stood waiting while the wound was cleansed. "Think of what you've lived through already," Philippe said to Jules. "Think of all the cold winter nights you've survived, trudging through the deep snow. You can make it. You are tough, tough as that billy goat of yours. What's his name? What do you call him?"

"Perdant," Jean-Paul said, chuckling. The others glanced at the policeman, who was slumped against a wall, useless.

Perdant looked up. The scoundrel had named a billy goat after him? That probably wasn't a compliment.

"How could you?" Céleste directed her ire at the policeman, who had his hands tucked into his armpits where he leaned on the wall. "Shooting a little boy like that?" She turned away from him and went to the window, where she stared out, trying to control her anger.

"It was an accident," Perdant said weakly. He was dizzy. He had to clench his teeth to keep them from chattering. But he'd been looking around. He had figured out a few things. Those Scouts, for instance. He had taken a good look at them, and it had begun to dawn on him who they really were. That Jean-Paul. He was one of the people Perdant suspected of forging papers. The redhead—Philippe, his name was. Wasn't he supposed to be in jail? The girl—he didn't know what she'd been doing here, but it had probably been illegal. There was that yellow suitcase full of contraband. And the multiple bootprints on the dusty floor—*those* hadn't escaped his attention.

But now these people were saving the life of the boy he had shot. And he was grateful. But he knew something they did not: The police were on their way. He didn't know what to do with that knowledge.

"Jules shared his meal with me one cold winter's night," Philippe was saying. "He said he was king of this château. Said he'd played here back when he was a kid."

From her place by the window, Céleste said, "As if he isn't still a kid. Or should be."

Philippe glanced over his shoulder at her. "Jules told me he knew the secret of this place. And that he'd show me."

"What did that mean?" Jean-Paul said. "And give me one of those bandages."

Philippe handed him a bandage and watched as Jean-Paul expertly began to wrap the boy's chest. "Jules," he said softly. "Hey. What's the secret?"

Jules heard all this as if from a far distance. *I do know its secret*, he wanted to tell them. *I know something important about this château*. But the words didn't reach his mouth.

Philippe looked up at Perdant and said, "This boy is worth a dozen of you. If he dies . . ."

Philippe didn't finish his sentence, but Perdant knew what he'd wanted to say: "I'll kill you." It's too late for that, Perdant thought. I am as good as dead. He already knew too much and had seen too much. Had put two and two together. His life was not worth much now.

The question was: What should he do with what was left of it?

»» ««

Perdant became aware of a rumbling vibration under his feet: Cars. Motorcycles.

"You should get out," he said, "all of you—now!"

Heads turned toward Perdant, and then toward the door, as the policeman pushed it open. The sound of car and motorcycle engines muscled its way into the chateau.

Perdant stepped outside and walked down the steps. Glancing down, he noticed the dark bloodstain on the lighter gravel. He rubbed at it with his foot, then noticed that the trail stretched all the way down the gravel drive and onto the road he had walked with Jules.

A jumble of cars and motorcycles roared through the open gate—why hadn't he at least closed the gate? It would have given him another minute to think. But no, in they drove, tires crunching on the gravel, parking helter-skelter. Car doors flew open and policemen and gendarmes leaped out. Seeing the blood-soaked Perdant, they drew their guns and took cover.

Perdant waved a hand at them, dismissing their concern. "There's no danger!" he shouted. "Put your guns away."

While the others put away their weapons, the senior police officer approached Perdant. "You're hurt!" he said.

"You should see the other fellow," Perdant said, making a weak joke. "I'm fine," he added, although he felt like he might vomit.

"Where *is* the other fellow?" the police captain asked.

Perdant indicated the trail of blood leading away, and the policeman directed a few gendarmes to follow the blood trail, then others to search around the outside of the château. Perdant stood helplessly watching. He felt as transparent as the spiderwebs that draped over the fields, as ephemeral as the dew that made them shimmer in the early-morning sun.

"What about in there?" the police officer said, nodding at the château. "Anyone in there?"

Inside the chateau, Jules was thinking of sunlight, the peculiar flickering sunlight of the forest, filtered through gently swaying pine boughs. He knew how to get from here to there, to that light. He'd done it before, and he wanted to tell his friends the way. He could hear the others talking, and he tried to bring the words from his mind to his mouth. But they wouldn't come.

He felt the calm, steady hands of Jean-Paul bandaging his chest and heard Jean-Paul quietly telling the others to "go the back way. All of you."

He heard the scrape of feet on the floor, the quiet jangle of buckles as rucksacks were hoisted onto shoulders, a suitcase being snapped shut. Words were spoken in hoarse whispers, and a strange calm pervaded the room.

"That's not going to work," Céleste said, her voice drifting over from near the window. "There are gendarmes prowling everywhere. They're surrounding the château."

Jules wanted to say the words that clung to his mind but wouldn't make the journey to his throat. What he knew about the château.

"We have false papers now," one of the Scouts was saying. "Maybe we can talk our way out of it."

"You have your real papers, too. Unless you want to burn them?"

"But we have to have our real papers for when we get to Switzerland! If we only have French identities, they will send us back to France."

"And, anyway, Perdant knows who you are," Céleste reminded them.

Go to the cellar, and find the wall that looks like a wall but is really a door. I can show you how it opens, Jules wanted to say, but it seemed he needed chest muscles to talk—even his feeble whisper sent ripples of bright pain through the agony that consumed him. *The hidden door in the cellar leads to a passage that turns into a tunnel. In the tunnel we will have to go one by one, feeling along with our hands, and follow it farther and farther, then up and up until the tunnel opens into a cave, a cave deep in the forest. But first, we only have to go down the stairs,*

Jules wanted to say, tasting the words on his tongue, *the stairs just there, around that corner.*

"Maybe there's somewhere we can hide," one of the boys was saying, but Jules knew there was not a closet or even a door to hide behind. No, there was only one way out, and he was the only one who knew it. His friends had saved his life. Now he needed to save theirs. He pried open his eyes and then his mouth, took a breath, and, despite the pain, managed a raspy croak that got the room's attention. In the silence that followed, he pushed out the words, "I know a way out."

➤➤ ◄◄

With a dozen policemen behind him, Perdant once again stood in front of the château doors. Worn bare of paint and touched by the first rays of morning sun, the gray wood gleamed like silver. Like the gates to heaven, he imagined.

Then the police captain pushed open the doors and the policemen poured into the château and began their hunt. They raced down the corridors, poked into rooms, disappearing into the shadowy darkness. Perdant stayed in the foyer. He felt the emptiness of the place—felt it all the way to the core of his being. A cool breeze whistled through the rooms and through him, carrying away the last shreds of his former self.

The abandoned rooms, the dim, unfurnished recesses, the gaping hole in the roof through which sunlight now streamed, the hollow echo of the policemen's voices calling to one another. He knew there was no one to find.

Were they ever here at all, or had he dreamed them? No,

they'd been here, infusing the place with light, filling the space with their energy and passion and something that he now recognized as hope. Where were they now?

Somehow they had gotten out.

He imagined them by now moving among the pines, their feet silent on the forest floor, Jules carried along in someone's arms as sunlight dappled the path ahead, showing them the way.

EPILOGUE

THE REAL PEOPLE WHO INSPIRED THIS STORY

This story is based on the true story of Le Chambon-sur-

Lignon and nearby villages in south central France, where the pastors, teachers, villagers, and a number of teenagers helped shelter and sometimes smuggle to safety possibly thousands of war refugees along with Jewish children and teens rescued from French concentration camps.

The character of Philippe was inspired by **Pierre Piton**, who came to Le Chambon at the age of seventeen. He enrolled at the unique private high school, L'Ecole

PIERRE PITON

Nouvelle Cévenole (see page 292), but soon got involved in clandestine work, which left him little time to study. He was first put to work bringing refugees to farms around the plateau, and often used his sled to transport their things and then himself back to the village.

Pierre then became a *passeur*, a people smuggler. Wearing his Scout uniform, he helped refugees get over the border to Switzerland. The "rules" as they are stated in this story, the route, and the circumstances of Philippe's arrest and release are based on Pierre's experiences. After his release from prison he returned to Le Chambon and continued to be involved in resistance work, although not as a *passeur*. Or at least not very often.

Little is known about what happened to him after the war, except that he kept moving—all the way to Africa, where he helped local people set up businesses.

LEFT TO RIGHT:
NELLY TROCMÉ,
MARCO DARCISSAC, AND
CATHERINE CAMBESSÉDÈS

Céleste was inspired by **Catherine Cambessédès Colburn**, who carried a number of messages for the *maquis*. She and her family were from Paris but always spent their summers in Le Chambon and were there on June 22, 1940, when France capitulated to Nazi Germany. Catherine still vividly recalls the declaration that Pastor André Trocmé (Pastor Autin) and Pastor Edouard Theis pronounced the next day, a Sunday.

Catherine's father returned to Paris after the vacation, but her mother and three of her siblings stayed in Le Chambon for two years, and Catherine attended L'Ecole Nouvelle Cévenole, the private high school. "I bloomed and blossomed with that system," she says, remembering her experience there. It was very different from typical French schools that were heavy on discipline and "used ridicule to achieve results."

Although she says she was quite afraid and therefore "not very good at it," she began to carry messages, contraband, and money for the *maquis*. The adventures of the character Céleste—traveling by train and bus to deliver a message, having to swallow the message, and experiencing a bombing—are based on Catherine's recollections of her experiences, as is the nighttime tandem bicycle ride and sleeping in a grotto full of *maquisards*. Céleste's experience with the suitcase almost being carried away on a flatcar is also based on Catherine's own recollections.

After the war Catherine studied at the Sorbonne in Paris but secured a scholarship to Mills College in California. She met her husband in California, where she raised a family, taught French at Stanford University, and then private lessons until recently.

OSCAR ROSOWSKY, WEARING THE JACKET IN WHICH PAPERS COULD BE HIDDEN

Due to a Vichy law preventing Jews from studying or working in law, medicine, and many other professions, *Oscar Rosowsky* (Jean-Paul) was not allowed to attend medical school. Instead, he got a job as an office equipment repairman in Nice. This gave him access to the local prefect's office, its typewriter, and the prefect's official stamp. He was seventeen when he forged a letter requesting the release of his mother from the Rivesaltes internment camp. It worked, and mother and son reunited in Nice. They heard the Le Chambon plateau was a safe place and decided to go there. By this time Oscar had changed his name to Jean-Claude Pluntz, and later to Jean-Claude Plunne.

On the plateau, Oscar and his mother lived apart—it was safer that way. Oscar lived for a time at Beau Soleil, a boardinghouse for high school students. There he became friends with the other residents who had some experience forging identity cards and other official papers. Together they set up a full-time forgery operation.

They realized the operation should be moved from their boardinghouse, and Oscar found a suitable place at the farm of Henri and Emma Héritier. There the young forger was able to turn out up to fifty documents a week. When raids were imminent, his forgery materials were hidden in a couple of unoccupied beehives.

Frenchmen at the time carried a half dozen documents, including an identity card, a military booklet, a certificate of demobilization, a work certificate, and ration cards for food, clothing, and other items, as well as the extra documents Oscar dubbed "plausibility papers." He was delighted to get his own "plausibility paper" when a policeman stopped him one night and gave him a ticket for riding his bicycle without a light.

Still hoping to become a doctor, Oscar forged himself a medical student ID and began taking classes at the university. One day, German police emptied the classrooms and searched students. Unfortunately, Oscar was carrying forged documents in the secret pockets built into his jacket. Although he almost escaped down a back stairway, as in Jean-Paul's story, Oscar was searched but ultimately saved thanks to a tin of throat lozenges. He kept the little box his whole life.

After the war, Oscar completed medical school and became

HANNE AND MAX IN SWITZERLAND IN THE FALL OF 1944

a doctor. He lived in Paris, where he also served as president of the General Medical Council of France.

When they were teenagers, **_Hanne Hirsch and Max Liebmann_** (Henni and Max) were deported from Germany to Gurs, a French concentration camp. There they met and fell in love. Hanne was rescued from the camp by the OSE (Oeuvre de Secours aux Enfants) and brought to Le Chambon when she was seventeen years old. She, along with seven others who'd also come from Gurs, lived at La Guespy (the Wasps' Nest). In August 1942, her mother, who was still being held in the camp, became ill and sent for her. By the time Hanne arrived, her mother was about to be deported, along with a thousand other detainees. Hanne walked nineteen kilometers to the freight yard and slept on the street overnight for a chance to see her. A gendarme who helped Hanne told her, "What goes on here tears my heart out." Hanne was able to spend about an hour with her mother before the train left. The last vestige Hanne saw of her was a little white handkerchief waving through the slats of the boxcar door.

From there, Hanne, who was traveling without false papers, took a train to see Max, who had been released from Gurs not long before and was staying at a Jewish Boy Scout camp. Hanne barely missed the ID check on the train, having fallen asleep on a pile of canvas mailbags in the mail car.

The camp had so far been tolerated, but its situation was becoming more tenuous. Hanne told Max, "If you're not safe here, come to Le Chambon."

After Hanne returned to Le Chambon, there were raids. Hanne hid in the woods with other young people from La Guespy and L'Abric, another house sheltering children. Because the raids continued for three weeks, the children and young people were taken to farms where they would be safer. Hanne stayed at two different farms. At the first one, she and the other girl sheltered there had to hide in a specially rigged woodpile when the gendarmes came searching. At the second farm, the two girls hid in an upstairs armoire (a freestanding closet) while a gendarme talked to the farmer on the first floor. From her hiding place, Hanne could hear the conversation downstairs.

"Are you hiding any Jews?" the gendarme asked.

"I'm not hiding anybody," the farmer said. "And I don't know what Jews look like."

The gendarme went on his way.

Max was still staying at the Scout Camp when they were warned there would be raids. When the leaders of the camp failed to provide safe haven for Max and a few others, Max and another young man made their way to Le Chambon as per Hanne's suggestion.

There Max ran into Hanne by chance. When he whistled at her, she ignored him until her friend made her turn around.

Max, age twenty-one, was sheltered in a hayloft at a farm for about three weeks before he was supplied with false papers obtained for him by Mireille Philip (see page 284), and in September 1942, he made for the border, hiking over the high mountains into Switzerland. Somewhere in the mountains, he buried his false identification card as he'd been requested to do—this was to protect the rescue operation in Le Chambon—fully knowing that without an ID, he could not go back to France.

Then, on the way down the mountain, he was caught by Swiss border police and taken to a mountain hostel where thirty others were also being detained. The next morning, the guard told them they would all have to go back to France.

As the detainees headed back up the mountain toward the border, one of the guards following behind shouted instructions at them. "Do *not* come back to Switzerland!" he yelled, then continued telling them what they should *not* do. Max realized that what the man was saying *not* to do was exactly what he *should* do to get safely into Switzerland.

After the patrol left, he told the group his idea, but only one other person was willing to try it. The others returned to France, but Max and his new friend reentered Switzerland safely.

HANNE'S FALSE IDENTIFICATION CARD

In February 1943, it was Hanne's turn to try for Switzerland. Thanks to her Swiss aunt, she had an entrance visa, but it was not possible to procure an exit visa from France. She was given false papers, and, dressing herself in layers of clothes rather than taking a telltale suitcase, she set off by train and eventually by foot to cross into Switzerland, where she was able to reunite with Max.

After the war, Hanne learned her mother had perished in Auschwitz. Max's parents also perished there.

Hanne and Max married in Switzerland, had a daughter, and moved to the United States in 1948. They still live in a suburb of New York City, and Hanne has spoken often about her experiences. Max and Hanne also contributed to the 2017 exhibit *Conspiracy of Goodness: How French Protestants Saved Thousands of Jews During WWII* at the Kupferberg Holocaust Center at Queensborough Community College, Queens, New York.

They tell their own stories here: http://khc.qcc.cuny.edu /goodness/reflect/hanne-and-max/.

And here: https://collections.ushmm.org/search/catalog /irn506661.

PAUL MAJOLA

Jules "La Crapule" (the scoundrel) is an entirely fictional character, although there was a young shepherd boy (aged ten to thirteen) named Paul Majola who delivered forged papers for Oscar Rosowsky (Jean-Paul) at night and in all types of weather.

Plainclothes officer ***Leopold Praly*** (Perdant) was a young policeman assigned to "maintain positive relationships with the locals," as well as to report their doings to the Vichy government via the regional prefect. Although he was probably less of a nuisance than Inspector Perdant in this story, he did make some arrests, including Jakob Lewin and his brother, Martin. Perdant's recollection of this event—of the young people surrounding the bus, singing, the gift of chocolate—is based on the recollections of those involved in the actual arrest as recorded by Renée Kann Silver, who was also sheltered as a child on the plateau.

Inspector Praly was shot and killed by *maquisards* on August 6, 1943, a scant eight months into his job in Le Chambon.

The events transpiring at the château on June 30 are entirely fictional. However, it is true that an escape route used in one of the guesthouses was through a secret door in the cellar into a tunnel that led to the forest.

THE ESCAPE ROUTE AT ONE OF THE HOUSES THAT SHELTERED JEWS

OTHERS IN THE STORY

Madeleine Dreyfus (Madame Desault) was a Jew from Paris, living in Lyons, who worked tirelessly rescuing children from French concentration camps through the OSE. She often brought two or three groups of children from the camps every week and took them to the farms and villages herself. At first the children were brought legally to the villages, but later they had to be brought clandestinely, already with false papers.

Eventually Madeleine was arrested by the Gestapo and deported to the Bergen-Belsen concentration camp. Although many people she worked with and many others working in the resistance died, Madeleine survived and returned to her husband and three children.

Mireille Philip (Madame Créneau) was sometimes referred to as "the Boss." She helped make false papers or arranged for people to get them. Official-looking stamps were carved into the bottoms of spools of thread she kept in her sewing basket. She and Pastor Theis established a rescue organization to help refugees get to Switzerland. Sometimes she took groups herself, traveling in the cabs of trains disguised in a coverall, her hair tucked up under a cap—everything covered in coal dust. She helped find safe places for refugees and eventually went to help the *maquis*, the armed French underground. "Be frightened, but keep going," she told her replacement. She did this while also raising five children by herself—her husband, André, was working for the French resistance in England with Charles de Gaulle.

Virginia Hall ("the American spy lady," as Claude describes her) is perhaps the unlikeliest character in the story. She was

VIRGINIA HALL

an American who worked for the British Special Operations Executive (SOE), a clandestine organization. She was sent to France and spent some time in the Haute-Loire region of France, which included the area around Le Chambon-sur-Lignon, organizing the resistance and coordinating parachute drops. She was a radio operator, who, when electricity was in short supply, rigged a bicycle to a generator to power her "suitcase radio." Jean Nallet, who joined the *maquis* while still a student at L'Ecole Nouvelle Cévenole, told of powering her transmitter by pedalling a stationary bicycle. Messages regarding parachute drops would come in codes like "the soup is hot" or "the shark has a soft nose."

As a result of an earlier hunting accident, she had a wooden leg with an aluminum foot. She named the leg Cuthbert and called the foot, in which she sometimes stored documents, her aluminum puppy.

Sometimes she disguised herself as an old French peasant woman with a herd of goats, which allowed her to limp about unnoticed on the plateau, making contacts and scouting parachute drop locations.

The Germans knew Virginia Hall as "the woman who limps" and considered her "the most dangerous Allied agent in France."

After the war, she married one of her *maquis* friends, returned to the United States, and joined the CIA. She retired at age sixty to a farm in Maryland where she raised, among other things, goats.

The Farmers

Most of the farms on the plateau were poor. Those farmers who sheltered children were given a small amount of money to help pay for doctor visits and incidentals. Often the real parents of the hidden children didn't know where their children were—it was safer that way. Madeleine Dreyfus would bring letters if she could when she visited to check on the children. Although in general the children were fed and cared for, not all of them had pleasant experiences at the farms, and all of them lived with fear and uncertainty. As one survivor said, "We were never children."

The Pastors

As well as encouraging their parishioners to engage in nonviolent forms of resistance, the Protestant pastors on the plateau were involved in the resistance in a variety of ways. André Trocmé and Edouard Theis sheltered and helped find shelter for Jewish children and refugees. Theis and another pastor, André Morel, smuggled them to Switzerland. Some pastors forged papers. The pastor of Freycenet received coded messages on his radio for the resistance. Another hid fake

**LEFT TO RIGHT: ÉDOUARD THEIS,
ROGER DARCISSAC (HEAD OF THE PUBLIC SCHOOL),
AND ANDRÉ TROCMÉ INSIDE THE INTERNMENT
CAMP AT SAINT-PAUL EYJEAUX**

ration cards in books in his library until they could be exchanged for authentic ration cards. The pastor in Le Mazet organized a group of Scouts to help him smuggle a group of Jewish boys to Switzerland disguised as Scouts.

André Trocmé and Edouard Theis, the pastors in Le Chambon, were outspoken in their encouragement of nonviolent resistance. When asked by the authorities for a list of all the Jewish refugees in Le Chambon, Trocmé refused, saying, "We don't know what a Jew is. We only know human beings."

The sermon that Céleste recalls on her nighttime bicycle ride are Trocmé's and Theis's words, delivered the day after the Armistice that Germany and France signed on June 22, 1940. Trocmé was a charismatic catalyst, famous for his Christmas

Day stories. The one delivered at the Christmas service in this story is paraphrased from one of his stories in the book *Angels and Donkeys*, translated by his daughter, Nelly.

Much has been written about Pastor Trocmé and his wife, Magda, also renowned as a courageous and tenacious advocate for Jewish and other refugees. She also taught Italian at L'Ecole Nouvelle Cévenole while caring for a family of four and giving room and board to four more people to support the family budget.

Their daughter, Nelly Trocmé Hewett, a resident of the United States, has been a champion of the story of the plateau, speaking at schools, universities, libraries, museums and synagogues all over the country. She was an invaluable advisor in the telling of this story. (She is pictured as a teen with Catherine Cambessédès and Marco Darcissac on page 275).

Both Pastor Trocmé and Pastor Theis, along with the director of the public school, Roger Darcissac (Marco's father), were arrested by the Vichy police in February 1943. They were released in March of the same year. Shortly afterward, both pastors went into hiding.

Some of the pastors used coded messages to let one another know that refugees were being sent their way. "I'm sending you two Old Testaments," a note might say, meaning two Jewish refugees were coming to the parsonage for help.

MANY OTHERS

Not only the area's Protestants were involved in these activities. Many of the plateau's Catholics, Jews, and agnostics were active participants, as well as its nonsectarian Darbyists (sometimes compared to Quakers or the Amish). L'Ecole Nouvelle Cévenole had many distinguished Jewish professors who had been ousted from their positions at universities in France, Austria, Poland, and Germany. With the aid of their colleagues, some continued to teach throughout the war, without taking false names.

Jewish refugees were also involved in the running of the children's homes. Emile Sèches, along with his wife, Solange, were proprietors of Tante Soly, the house right next door to the hotel where recuperating German soldiers were billeted. Emile Sèches was Jewish; Madame Sèches was Catholic. Some Jewish adults also stayed at local residences, including a rabbi who lived for three years at Beau Soleil.

Although scores of French citizens, convents, and churches all over France, as well as the Grand Mosque of Paris, sheltered Jews and Jewish children, it is important to recognize that the plateau of the Haute-Loire was unusual in the sheer scale of its involvement, and in its universal commitment to this cause.

How was this possible? Were there no informants? Perhaps because of their background as Huguenots with a history of persecution, its citizens were sympathetic to other persecuted people. Aided by their taciturn nature, the inhabitants kept quiet. Even the children knew to be quiet. When two young Jewish girls who had once been friends in Germany ran into each other in the village of Le Chambon, neither girl said a word of greeting or acknowledged the other.

There were many, many remarkable and courageous people, both adults and young people, who were actively involved in resistance activities—I regret I can't name them all. If you would like to find out more, please refer to the bibliography.

GURS INTERNMENT CAMP

CONCENTRATION CAMPS

During World War II, concentration camps rose "like mushrooms after a rain," according to Himmler, Germany's second-in-command. There were labor camps, POW camps, collection and transit camps, internment, and extermination camps—all of them different kinds of concentration camps.

Although we often think of concentration camps as being located only in Germany and Poland, there were dozens of them in France. Even though none of these were extermination camps, hundreds of people died in them from disease, starvation, exposure, or execution. Of the 340,000 Jews living in France at the start of the war, 75,000 were deported to extermination camps, where 72,500 were killed.

THE BOY SCOUTS IN FRANCE

The German occupiers had a complicated relationship with youth sporting organizations, including the Scouts, which is what the Boy Scouts were called in France. These organizations were very popular before and during the war, with three million enrolled youths, ages fourteen to twenty.

JAKOB LEWIN ABOUT TO LEAVE FOR SWITZERLAND DISGUISED AS A FRENCH BOY SCOUT. HE AND HIS BROTHER, MARTIN, WERE ARRESTED BY OFFICER PRALY. JAKOB WAS RELEASED SHORTLY AFTERWARD. MARTIN WAS SENT TO GURS AND EVENTUALLY MADE IT BACK TO LE CHAMBON.

Scouting was forbidden in the northern occupied zone of France, as it was considered a way for young men to train for resistance activities. Even so, it was tolerated in the south, and a Scout uniform was thought to be a good disguise by the resistance.

Many of the young men who joined the *maquis* had been Boy Scouts, with helpful training in outdoor living and survival techniques. Often, they used their Scout names, such as Ostrich, Giraffe, Otter, and so on, as code names in the *maquis*.

THE SCHOOL
AND GUESTHOUSES

Young people from all over Europe came to Le Chambon both as students and as refugees. They attended the public school or

**SNOWBALL FIGHT OUTSIDE ONE OF THE HOMES RUN
BY SWISS AID FOR CHILDREN**

**LE CHAMBON STREET (A POPULAR SLEDDING ROUTE),
PROBABLY THE WINTER OF 1941–42**

the private high school, L'Ecole Nouvelle Cévenole, founded in 1938 by Pastors André Trocmé and Edouard Theis with an innovative educational mission of teaching peace, nonviolence, internationalism, foreign languages, sports, and artistic expression. The school was coeducational, and the honor system prevailed. Students from out of town and refugees stayed in guesthouses in the village.

In its early years there was no dedicated school building. Classes took place in any available spaces: an empty hotel room, at the church, in an attic, in the basement of the pharmacy, in the kitchen of one of the teachers, and even in the large bathroom of Le Colombier, a residence for girls attending the high school.

**A MIX OF LOCAL AND JEWISH TEENAGERS
IN LE CHAMBON, WINTER 1943–44**

The area attracted tourists and those seeking the clean air and healthy food of the high plateau. Thus, Le Chambon and the surrounding villages were well equipped to host children and other refugees, with thirty-eight guesthouses and eleven children's hostels that could be called into service, as well as a number of hotels.

Even today, Le Chambon is still welcoming refugees.

Yad Vashem World Holocaust Remembrance Center has awarded Israel's highest civilian honor, the Righteous Among the Nations, to more than ninety individuals on the plateau. The Diplôme d'Honneur, awarded by Yad Vashem, "pays homage to the inhabitants of Le Chambon-sur-Lignon and to the neighboring communes for coming to the assistance of Jews . . . from 1940–1944. Obeying their conscience, they put their own lives in danger by welcoming persecuted Jews into their homes and by providing for their needs thanks to their love for their fellow man."

No one kept track, and so no one knows how many Jews were sheltered on or passed through the plateau. The most agreed-upon estimate is about 3,500.

Mr Minister:

We have learned of the scenes of horror that took place three weeks ago in Paris, when the French police, under orders of the occupying forces, arrested all Jewish families in their homes and then interned them in the *Vél' d'Hiv*. Fathers were taken from their families and deported to Germany, children taken from their mothers, who met the same fate as their husbands. Knowing from experience that the decrees of the occupying forces, are, in short order, imposed upon non-occupied France, where they are presented as spontaneous decision of the Head of the French State, we fear that deportation measures against Jews will soon be applied in the southern zone. We would like to inform you that there are, among us, a certain number of Jews. However, we do not distinguish between Jews and non-Jews. It is contrary to the teachings of the Gospel.

If our comrades, whose only fault is to have been born in another religion, receive the order to be deported or even counted, they will disobey the order, and we will do everything to hide them.

**A TRANSLATION OF THE LETTER WRITTEN
BY STUDENTS TO GEORGES LAMIRAND,
YOUTH MINISTER FOR THE VICHY GOVERNMENT**

HISTORICAL TIMELINE*

1934   Hitler becomes Chancellor of Germany, systematically begins eroding rights of Jews.

1938

NOV. 9–10   *Kristallnacht*—Jewish businesses and synagogues in Germany destroyed, 30,000 men arrested, at least 100 killed.

1939   Germany invades Czechoslovakia, Poland, Denmark, Norway, Netherlands, Belgium, Luxembourg.

Great Britain, New Zealand, Australia and France declare war on Germany.

1940

MAY   Geman army enters France.

JUNE 22   France capitulates; armistice (an agreement to cease hostilities) signed between France and Germany, Germany occupies the northern half of France. The southern half of France remains unoccupied but under the governance of French leader Marshal Philippe Pétain, who feels it is in France's interest to collaborate with Nazi Germany.

JULY 1   Pétain's government moves to Vichy in the southern, unoccupied zone of France and begins to enact policies copied from Nazi laws and ordinances, including those restricting the rights of Jews and others.

SEPT. 27   Germany starts census of Jews in occupied zone of France.

OCT. 3   Vichy enacts first *Statut des Juifs*, banning Jews from certain professions, including medicine, law, journalism, commercial and industrial jobs.

1941

MAR.–NOV.   The Vichy government enacts increasingly harsher restrictions on Jews, including authorizing confiscation of Jewish property.

MAY   Guesthouses in Le Chambon begin to take in children rescued from camps.

JUNE 22   Germany begins invasion of Russia.

DEC. 7–8   Japanese bomb Pearl Harbor; U.S. declares war on Japan.

DEC. 11   Germany declares war on the U.S.

1942

MAR. 1   Allies begin bombing of France

MAR. 27   First train of Jews leaves Drancy (internment camp in northern France) for Auschwitz extermination camp in Poland.

MAY 29   Jews in occupied zone, six years old and up, ordered to wear a yellow star.

JULY 16–17   Round-up of Jews in Paris and sent to the "Vel d'Hiv" stadium. Nearly 13,000 people, including children, were arrested and deported to Auschwitz and other Nazi concentration camps.

AUG. First raids by French police on Le Chambon

AUG. 5 Start of deportations from southern zone of France to Auschwitz and other concentration and extermination camps in Poland and Germany.

AUG. 13 Switzerland closes all of its borders to Jewish refugees.

NOV. 8 Allies begin invasion of North Africa

NOV. 11 Germans invade and occupy southern zone of France. The whole of France is now occupied by Germany.

DEC. Police officer Praly arrives in Le Chambon.

Convalescing German soldiers are biletted in a local hotel in Le Chambon.

1943

JAN. 24 Germans destroy the old port of Marseilles (in southern France).

FEB. 13 Pastors Trocmé and Theis and public school director Roger Darcissac are arrested in Le Chambon.

FEB. 25 Officer Praly conducts first raid in Le Chambon.

MAR. 15–16 The pastors and school director are released, Trocmé goes into hiding.

JUNE 29 Plainclothes German police conduct a raid on the House of Rocks, one of the guesthouses in Le Chambon, arresting the director and eighteen students—all sent to various Nazi concentration camps.

JULY 9   Allies reach Sicily.

AUG. 6   Officer Praly shot and killed by the resistance in Le Chambon

1944

JUNE 6   D-Day landings in Normandy, on the northern coast of France, beginning the campaign to liberate northern Europe from German occupation.

AUG. 15   French and Allied troops land in Provence (in southern France), marking the beginning of progressive liberation of France by Allies, French armies and Resistance.

AUG. 24–25   The liberation of Paris. Germans surrender.

SEPT. 1   French forces reach le Chambon.

1945

MAY 7   Germany surrenders to the Allies, ending the war in Europe.

SEPT. 2   Japan surrenders to the Allies, ending the war in Asia.

* This timeline is based on actual historical events.

BIBLIOGRAPHY

* Recommended for young readers

**Books or documentaries specifically concerning Le Chambon-sur-Lignon and its residents

***Recommended for young readers and specifically concerning Le Chambon-sur-Lignon and its residents

BOOKS

Camus, Albert. *Notebooks 1942–1951*. Translated by Justin O'Brien. New York: Alfred A. Knopf, 1965.

***Durland DeSaix, Deborah, and Karen Gray Ruelle. *Hidden on the Mountain: Stories of Children Sheltered from the Nazis in Le Chambon.* New York: Holiday House, 2007.

* Greenfeld, Howard. *The Hidden Children*. Boston: Houghton-Mifflin, 1993.

**Grose, Peter. *A Good Place to Hide: How One French Village Saved Thousands of Lives During World War II.* New York: Pegasus Books, 2015.

**Hallie, Philip. *Lest Innocent Blood Be Shed: The Story of the Village of Le Chambon and How Goodness Happened There.* New York: Harper Perennial, 1979.

Halls, W. D. *The Youth of Vichy France.* Oxford, UK: Clarendon Press, 1981.

Johnson, Eric A., and Karl-Heinz Reuband. *What We Knew: Terror, Mass Murder, and Everyday Life in Nazi Germany; an Oral History.* New York: Basic Books, 2005.

Kaminsky, Sarah. *Adolfo Kaminsky: A Forger's Life*. Los Angeles: DoppelHouse Press, 2016.

**Kann Silver, Renée, and Connie Colker Steiner. *And Yet, I Still Loved France: Memoir of a European Childhood*. Rego Park, NY: Marble House Editions, 2012. (Renée's and her sister's WWII experiences include a stay at a farm on the plateau.)

Kedward, H. R. *In Search of the Maquis: Rural Resistance in Southern France, 1942–1944*. Oxford, UK: Clarendon Press, 1993.

Lazare, Lucien. *Rescue as Resistance: How Jewish Organizations Fought the Holocaust in France*. New York: Columbia University Press, 1996.

* Leapman, Michael. *Witnesses to War: Eight True-life Stories of Nazi Persecution*. New York: Viking, 1998.

**Lecomte, François. Translated by Jacques P. Trocmé. *I Will Never Be Fourteen Years Old: Le Chambon-sur-Lignon & My Second Life*. Wayne, PA: Beach Lloyd, 2009.

Lowrie, Donald A. *The Hunted Children*. New York: W. W. Norton, 1963.

***Matas, Carol. *Greater Than Angels*. New York: Simon Pulse, 1999.

Samuel, Vivette. *Rescuing the Children: A Holocaust Memoir*. Madison, WI: University of Wisconsin Press, 2002.

Stroud, Dean G., ed. *Preaching in Hitler's Shadow: Sermons of Resistance in the Third Reich*. Grand Rapids, MI: Wm. B. Eerdmans, 2013.

Trocmé, André. *Angels and Donkeys: Tales for Christmas and Other Times*. Translated by Nelly Trocmé Hewett. Intercourse, PA: Good Books, 1998.

Weitz, Margaret Collins. *Sisters in the Resistance: How Women Fought to Free France, 1940–1945*. New York: John Wiley & Sons, 1995.

FILM AND TELEVISION DOCUMENTARIES

L'oeil de Vichy (The Eye of Vichy). Directed by Claude Chabrol, FIT Production (Firm), Institut national de l'audiovisuel (France), TF1 Films Production, First-Run Features Home Video (Firm) (Film release, 1993; DVD release, 2003).

The Sorrow and the Pity. Directed by Marcel Ophuls. 1969; Chatsworth, CA: Milestone Film & Video, 2001. DVD.

***Weapons of the Spirit*. Directed by Pierre Sauvage. 1989; Chambon Foundation, remastered 2014. The 2019 thirtieth-anniversary edition and abridged classroom version is available at www.chambon.org/weapons_en.htm.

EXHIBIT

***Conspiracy of Goodness: How French Protestants Rescued Thousands of Jews During WWII*. Exhibit at the Kupferberg Holocaust Center, Queensborough Community College, Queens, NY. Fall 2017. On view on the website: khc.qcc.cuny.edu.

MUSEUM

***Lieu de Mémoire au Chambon (A Place of Memory);* Le Chambon-sur-Lignon, France, www.memoireduchambon.com/en/.

IMAGE CREDITS

Page 274 © *AD Haute-Loire.*

Page 275 courtesy Catherine Cambessédès Colburn.

Page 276 Peter Grose: Private Collection.

Page 278 Private Collection of Hanne and Max Liebmann.

Page 281 Private Collection of Hanne and Max Liebmann (donated to the United States Holocaust Memorial Museum).

Page 282 *Weapons of the Spirit* (Chambon Foundation).

Page 285 © *Fonds privé.*

Page 287 © *Fonds Darcissac/Commune du Chambon-sur-Lignon.*

Page 290 United States Holocaust Memorial Museum, courtesy of Hanna Meyer-Moses.

Page 291 United States Holocaust Memorial Museum, courtesy of Jack Lewin.

Page 292 *Weapons of the Spirit* (Chambon Foundation).

Page 293 © *Fonds Darcissac/Commune du Chambon-sur-Lignon.*

Page 294 *Weapons of the Spirit* (Chambon Foundation).

Page 295 courtesy of Lieu de Memoire.

ACKNOWLEDGMENTS

First and foremost, I am indebted to those who shared their stories with me, including Max and Hanne Liebmann, Renée Kann Silver, Catherine Cambessédès Colburn, Rolande Lombard, and Nelly Trocmé Hewett, all of whom lived or were sheltered on the plateau during the War. My thanks and apologies for whatever I got wrong.

Both Rolande and Nelly described sledding down the main street despite the disapproval of the *garde champêtre*, as well as other "folkloric details," as Nelly put it. It was one of Nelly's brothers who, when he went to buy food from the farms, brought along a frying pan and matches. Too hungry to make it all the way home, he would stop and cook himself a snack. Nelly herself confesses to sneaking spoonfuls of chestnut "paste" (sweetened pureed chestnuts) from the pantry.

Nelly also gave me a kind of letter of introduction to the good people of Le Chambon-sur-Lignon, where my traveling companions and I toured the *Lieu de Mémoire* (Memorial museum) with city councilor Denise Vallat; met mayor Madame Wauquiez-Mott; viewed an exhibit at the train station with Claire Souvignet; peeked in on Oscar Rosowsky's room at the former Héretier farm; got a tour of "La Guespy," the house where Hanne lived; took a dip in the Lignon; and got lost in the woods.

All of this (including getting lost) was thanks to my ex-pat cousin, Joel Preus, who served as driver, translator, interpreter, aide-de-camp (and aide de camping), research assistant, manuscript critiquer, and steady supplier of laughs. He and his sister, *ma chère cousine* Mary, are always excellent companions. Joel and his wife Christine Lenfant, contributed advice about all things French, as well as many names (including Jules "La Crapule"). Another French-speaking relative, Catherine Preus, is responsible for the pronunciation guide. *Je vous dois une fière chandelle.*

Thank you to the many people who read and commented on early drafts—including Nelly Trocmé Hewett, numerous relatives, and many Duluth and Atsokan Island writer friends who read all or part of the manuscript in various states of disarray. *Comment puis-je vous remercier?*

I would also like to thank others who have told this story before me and who generously helped me locate photos and offered information, including Karen Ruelle and Debra De-Saix, authors of *Hidden on the Mountain*, and Pierre Sauvage and his enlightening documentary *Weapons of the Spirit.* Look for the 2019 thirtieth-anniversary edition of the remastered documentary, along with an abridged classroom version. Thank you, too, to Peter Grose for his excellent book *A Good Place to Hide*, for permission to use his translation of the "rules" recited to those who were smuggled to Switzerland, and for the photo and story of Oscar Rosowsky's jacket, as well as many other stories you can find in his book.

As ever, a big *merci beaucoup* to my agent, Stephen Fraser, and a *grosse bise* to everyone at Amulet/Abrams who made this book happen: Hana Anouk Nakamura, Evangelos Vasilakis, Marie Oishi, Emily Daluga, Sara Sproull, and S. M. Vidaurri for the evocative illustrations. To my patient editor, Howard Reeves, *mes sincères remerciements.*

To those whom I have forgotten, my apologies, and *merci beaucoup.*

OTHER BOOKS OF INTRIGUE AND ADVENTURE BY MARGI PREUS

HEART OF A SAMURAI

Newbery Honor book
New York Times bestseller
NPR Backseat Book Club pick

★ "It's a classic fish-out-of-water story (although this fish goes into the water repeatedly), and it's precisely this classic structure that gives the novel the sturdy bones of a timeless tale."

—*Booklist*, starred review

★ "Capturing his wonder, remarkable willingness to learn, the prejudice he encountered and the way he eventually influenced officials in Japan to open the country, this highly entertaining page-turner . . . is a captivating . . . retelling of the boy's adventures."

—*Kirkus Reviews*, starred review

★ "Stunning debut novel. Preus places readers in the young man's shoes, whether he is on a ship or in a Japanese prison. Her deftness in writing is evident in two poignant scenes, one in which Manjiro realizes the similarities between the Japanese and the Americans and the other when he reunites with his Japanese family."

—*School Library Journal*, starred review

WEST OF THE MOON

★ "Like dun silk shot through with gold, Preus interweaves the mesmerizing tale of Astri's treacherous and harrowing mid-nineteenth-century emigration to America with bewitching tales of magic."

—*Booklist*, starred review

★ "History, fiction and folklore intertwine seamlessly in this lively, fantastical adventure and moving coming-of-age story."

—*Kirkus Reviews*, starred review

★ "Enthralling and unflinching, this historical tale resonates with mythical undertones that will linger with readers after the final page is turned."

—*School Library Journal*, starred review

★ "[A] fast-paced, lyrically narrated story, which features a protagonist as stalwart and fearless as any fairy-tale hero."

—*The Horn Book*, starred review

SHADOW ON THE MOUNTAIN

★ "Preus infuses the story with the good-natured humor of a largely unified, peace-loving people trying to keep their sanity in a world gone awry."

—*Kirkus Reviews*, starred review

★ "Preus masterfully weds a story of friendship with the complications faced by 14-year-old Espen and his friends as Nazi restrictions and atrocities become part of their everyday lives . . . This is at once a spy thriller, a coming-of-age story, and a chronicle of escalating bravery."

—*School Library Journal*, starred review

"A closely researched historical novel . . . relates this wartime tale with intelligence and humor . . . Ms. Preus deftly fuses together historical fact (Espen is based on a real-life spy) and elements of Norwegian culture to conjure a time and place not so terribly long ago."

—*The Wall Street Journal*

"The final chapters, which chronicle Espen's dramatic escape to Sweden . . . take the book into adventure-thriller territory without losing the humanity that characterizes Preus's account."

—*The Horn Book*

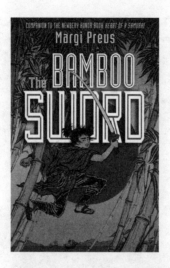

THE BAMBOO SWORD

★ "Middle-grade readers eager for adventure with a solid grounding in history will be enchanted."

— *Booklist*, starred review

"Thanks to the lively, warm, and witty storyteller's voice and the vivid, sensuous depictions of the katana swish and kimono swirl of 19th-century Japan, readers will feel immersed in this tumultuous time in Japanese history."

— *Kirkus Reviews*

Margi Preus is the author of the Newbery Honor book *Heart of a Samurai* and other books for young readers, which have been honored as ALA/ALSC Notable Children's Books, been selected by NPR Backseat Book Club, won multiple awards, and landed on the *New York Times* bestseller list. At home in Duluth, Minnesota, she likes to ski, hike, canoe, or sit quietly with a book in her lap.

Margi stumbled upon a snippet of this story when researching her World War II story *Shadow on the Mountain* and was captivated by the tale of the village where, when the gendarmes came hunting, the Jewish children hidden in their midst were sent into the forest to hide. When the danger passed, the village children sang a song to let their hidden friends know it was safe to come out of hiding.